W. O. MITCHELL'S
HOW I SPENT MY SUMMER HOLIDAYS

"BAWDY AND RAUNCHY.... Powerfully evocative prose.... An uncannily accurate feel for the emotional viewpoint of a 12-year-old boy."
—*The Globe and Mail*

"A MASTER OF PRAIRIE FICTION IS UP TO HIS OLD TRICKS."
—*Macleans*

"HE'S THE MOST LYRICAL... WRITER IN CANADA... with a tale that goes far deeper than his original Saskatchewan stories."
—*FM Guide*

"AN EXCELLENT BOOK... tightly plotted and morally complex."
—*Quill & Quire*

"TENSE AND UNUSUAL.... More complex and menacing than anything in his earlier books."
—*Toronto Star*

HOW I SPENT MY SUMMER HOLIDAYS

W. O. Mitchell

SEAL BOOKS
McClelland-Bantam, Inc.
Toronto

With gratitude to the English Department,
University of Windsor

*This low-priced Seal Book
has been completely reset in a type face
designed for easy reading, and was printed
from new plates. It contains the complete
text of the original hard-cover edition.*
NOT ONE WORD HAS BEEN OMITTED.

HOW I SPENT MY SUMMER HOLIDAYS

A Seal Book / published by arrangement with
Macmillan of Canada

PRINTING HISTORY

Macmillan of Canada edition published August 1981

*A Selection of Book-of-Month Club of Canada and
Literary Guild of Canada.*

Excerpted in Edmonton Magazine, *October 1981;* Calgary
Herald, *November 1981;* Athabasca University Magazine,
February-March 1982 and Interface Magazine.

*Seal edition / December 1982
2nd printing . . . May 1987*

Back cover photograph by John Reeves.

ISBN 0-7704-1780-9

PRINTED IN CANADA

U   11 10 9 8 7 6 5 4 3

for Hugh

ARMA VIRUMQUE CANO

HOW
I SPENT
MY SUMMER
HOLIDAYS

I

There have been times when I have almost caught it. I think. But always it has slipped away from me, leaving me with a feeling of loss and of sadness. There is apprehension, too, about what might be in it for me; I am not at all sure that I want to capture it; maybe I want it to escape me. Perhaps I ought to stop trying to trap it altogether, if I know what's good for me. Which I don't.

I have narrowed it down to the summer of 1924 and perhaps the winter of 1924-25. It has nothing to do with Sir Walter Raleigh School, Miss Coldtart's Grade Four and Five room, Mr. Mackey's Six and Seven and Eight room. The prairie cave Peter Deane-Cooper and I dug that summer, and the Mental swimming-hole in the Little Souris River, are both important to it, but they suggest only summer. Winter too belongs, which would naturally suggest the Arena, and I can hear rink echo all right, in the memory resonance.

I know this: it does concern King Motherwell and his wife, Bella. That's it! No closer! It's startled. It's gone. Possibly I may never capture it. I hope.

I have hoped so, ever since the stubborn dream began to visit me some ten years ago. It is not quite a nightmare, but it is close to one. Each time it has wakened me in the early morning hours, and after I have lost the dream quality of separation that sometimes softens the emotional commitment, I become more upset. In sleep I have been an uninvolved spectator. Awake I am revolted. I realize clearly now that I have just been in a large room in the charge of a stylishly dressed and vaguely middle-aged woman, who is conducting me on some sort of tour down a long line of white-sheeted

1

lumps. At first they suggest a devout rank of Moslem rears, their praying owners all facing Mecca. Too small, though. They have to be children's rumps. I have been given an invitation, not spoken—understood, and, since I am walking down this proffered row, I must have tacitly agreed to what is going on here.

Now I see that each of the white sheets has been parted—carefully—to reveal orifices, and I am looking at each of them in turn. There is an operating-room objectivity, yet not for humanitarian reasons; there is no mistaking the ominous intent here. They are child anuses, small and closed. Now they have opened like mushrooms to reveal their chocolate gills. Suddenly, cruelly, they have become caves. The woman has a kidney-shaped purse of leather, hanging down like a sporran before her, much like the one that Mr. Dowdy carried for change and bills and tickets when he drove the Snodgrass Bakery rig of Merle Morgan on his dairy rounds, or Charlie Jasper with the ice dray.

Thank God I do not buy her terrible tickets, for the exchange would be brothel-ugly, though she does not remind me at all of Sadie Rossdance and her three little cottages just beyond the Fairgrounds south-east of town. But why should the dream make me think of Miss Coldtart and of Mrs. Judge Hannah? Why should I think of my own mother?

It seems so long ago. It is as though I am listening to my own voice coming to me not just from my own past but from much beyond that and from quite another world, the age of Jason or of Ulysses or of Aeneas. We have been divinely created, for the Bible and Mrs. Judge Hannah told us so in Knox Presbyterian Sunday School. Hesiod could compare us to the pre-Aryan silver age heroes: "...eaters of bread, utterly subject to our mothers, however long they lived."

Lobbidy and the Liar and Peter Deane-Cooper and Angus Hannah and I and all the others never sacrificed to the Gods, though I'm not all that sure about Austin Musgrave. We did make deals with the Gods: Baptist, Methodist, Catholic, Lutheran, Presbyterian, Holy Roller, Anglican. "Oh God, get me through that exam tomorrow in percent and interest and capital and I will never smoke another Millbank or milkweed-stalk or dead-Virginia-creeper-leaf cigarette!" "Oh God, let me win the fight with Fat Isbister behind the school after four and I promise not to get Daisy Inwards to lift her skirt and pull down her pants to show it!" A good deal for us but a poor one from God's point of view, for "it" had been quite disappointing and nothing at all to see.

That age and the isolated rural village of my boyhood are long, long gone. Our town lay in the South Saskatchewan prairies, sixty miles north of the Montana border. The superlative sun that shone down on us was Greek; the grass sea around us was our Aegean. I was born there in 1912, the same year the town was born. By 1924 it had grown to almost five thousand people. If you included the population of the Provincial Mental Hospital.

The village I knew no longer lives. I look at the melanin spots like pear-skin bruises on the backs of my hands and I mourn Peck's bad boy; I wonder what the hell the "S" in William S. Hart's name stood for. Henty would have tough sledding today, and so would Horatio Alger, Jr., or Chums, or Conrad, or Mark Twain. I mourn the loss of an age of innocence.

The loss of my own innocence was not a simple event; it must have been an imperceptible corruption taking time. It had probably been well started when I saw the ad on a back page of *War Aces Magazine*, with the cartoon of a small boy smirking and leaning nonchalantly against a street wall, while a porter with a great trunk on his slant back struggled toward a hotel door. From the trunk lid there fanned up lines crying: "Let me out! Let me out!" The ad promised that if I sent my ten cents to Chicago, I would receive by return mail "Ventrillo," a magic instrument that would fit under my tongue and enable me to throw my voice just as well as the boy helping the porter with the trunk on his back.

"Ventrillo" turned out to be a disappointing disc of tin folded into a half-circle with a hole punched through both sides. I also received a postage-stamp-small booklet of faded pink, explaining that the instrument would assist me in doing bird-calls. I didn't even try. I had no desire to thrill my parents and friends with bird song. The booklet said that I had now undertaken with them a solemn contract never to reveal to anyone these ventriloquial secrets that the world-famous Vox Humana had entrusted to the "Ventrillo" people in Chicago. I too could become a great ventriloquist if I followed their instructions to the letter: "Without moving your lips, say the alphabet over and over while standing in front of a mirror." After a week of practice I still could not throw my voice, and I had discovered that only the most gifted and experienced of ventriloquists should attempt the following words: part and puck and, of course, punt.

My innocence crumbled more when I realized that in spite of detailed instruction from *A Thousand Things a Boy Can Do,* I would never be able to carve and steam and torque a boomerang that would ever come back to me. I never did get the opportunity to follow their advice under "Horses, Run-away, How To Stop," with the illustration of a boy soaring upwards like a ballet dancer to grab the bridle of a foam-flecked horse with eyeballs rolled back so that only their whites showed, but I'm certain I was saved from yet another broken adult promise to fertilize my growing cynicism. The events of the summer of 1924 accelerated the irreversible corruption of my innocence. That was the year I was twelve, and there should have been a rage in Heaven.

The village of my prairie boyhood was not really one unified community; it contained several societies distinct within the larger constellation. The largest and most dominant was adult of course, but our child society was real and separate, and we tried to keep it for our own. The other ones were slightly removed from the town itself: the Mental Hospital sodality to the east, and the one to the north-west that celebrated life out at Sadie Rossdance's three little cottages. That comes to four. I cannot recall any great flow of understanding among them.

Most important to me and the others in our child world was the Little Souris River, a wandering prairie vein, dark with earth flour, rushing and swollen with snow run-off in early spring, shrinking and slowing almost to stillness by mid-August. The river was ours, though it did seem undeserved, almost a miracle; for we knew that water ought to be earned by digging a well to find it, or a dug-out to capture it. In all seasons we were drawn to the river, less often for skating in winter, almost daily to swim during our summer holidays. Sundays—never.

We hardly ever went out singly, or even in pairs; we might start out that way, but by the town's edge we would be joined by others, and after the Fairgrounds, boys from the

south side of town had turned us into a true pilgrimage
making for the Mental hole or, farther upstream, the CPR
hole. It was not Canterbury so much as Mecca, for the prairie
air was desert dry in our Arab nostrils, and long before we
had reached the river we had taken off our blouses, to put
them over our heads with the sleeves tied behind our necks
as burnooses.

We did not often carry on beyond the river to the east
and Brokenshell Grove; that part of the river was seldom
used for secular purposes, just for Sunday-school picnics and
for the South Saskatchewan Holy Rollers' summer camp
meeting. For three weeks in July their great khaki tent would
be pitched in the grove while they testified and prayed and
converted and immersed in the river for spiritual cleansing.
Their tent often had a happy sound, with singing and piano
accompaniment exuberant as a tennis-ball bouncing down
stairs.

Sadie Rossdance's three cottages had a happy sound too;
there was also a piano in each of them.

*It was almost twenty years since I had been back there
when I returned for my town's fiftieth birthday in August of
1962. It was shocking to find that it had grown so, well
beyond Sadie Rossdance's and right out to the edge of the
Mental Hospital grounds. Yet so much had been condensed—
our own house, the distance from it to downtown, the Little
Souris River. I walked out Government Road, now surprisingly
paved, as far as the Mental Hospital. Those red-brick build-
ings seemed as large as I remembered them and the ground
plantings of poplar saplings, which had resembled slender
binder whips when I was a boy, had actually grown into tall
bluffs of trees.*

*I climbed under the barbed-wire fence and walked across
what had once been Muhlbier land. It was unchanged, for
whoever farmed it now kept it as pasture.*

*Even as I began to walk towards the river, I realized that
I was on a time return. It was the same wind as the wind of
boyhood, still careless in the prairie grass, like the braided
whisper that sighed restlessly through our classrooms. Maybe
it wasn't the wind but the grasshoppers, stirred by my feet to
leap ahead of me and drift sideways on the wind, that carried*

me with them in a memory loop back to Sir Walter Raleigh School. And Mr. Mackey.

For a moment it was difficult to find any relationship at all between our principal and grasshoppers, and then I remembered; consequences. *I did not like the word as a boy. Mr. Mackey did.*

"Any boy found carving his initials on the desks—any boy found on the school grounds in possession of a slingshot—any boy caught using the tin fire-escape as a plaything—will have to suffer the consequences." There it was: consequences were something to be *suffered;* our lives had been mined with them so that all pleasures must be followed by an explosion of unpleasant consequences.

At the beginning of each school year Mr. Mackey would line us up in the hallway, both sexes from Grade One to Grade Eight, to listen to his ant-and-grasshopper speech. After the grasshopper had wasted his summer in sloth and fun to die of starvation, Mr. Mackey went on to tell us of the ant society with its queen and warriors and workers and males and slaves, each caste with its own duty to perform. Each one of us too, he said, had his own obligation to the others.

Eight times I heard him explain that obligation formed a great ladder in our own society. Boys and girls were on the bottom rung. We had obligation to each other at work and at play; we owed it next to our family and parents, to our teachers and our school, then to our Province and its Premier, our country and its Prime Minister, William Lyon Mackenzie King, and the whole scarlet British Empire and our monarch. God stood on the top rung. Ascending this Aristotelian obligation ladder purified us, by refining us of all child matter. Mr. Mackey was there to see that we did not miss a single rung. Or else.

In the summer of 1924, we got a different slant on the ant and the grasshopper from King Motherwell, who owned the Royal Pool Hall. King had taken a swim with Lobbidy and Angus and Musgrave and Peter and me. We had come out to dry off in the early June sun and Lobbidy didn't realize till it was too late that he was sitting on an ant colony and got stung on both cheeks and the backs of his legs. When we had helped him brush the last ant off and he had dived in and come out again and picked another place to sit down and we had quit laughing, King said, "Which side are you fellows on, anyway? The grasshopper or the ant?"

That was an easy one for me to answer, because even when Mr. Mackey was giving his ant-and-grasshopper speech, I had secretly been pulling for the grasshopper. "Grasshopper."

"Ant," Musgrave said.

"Yeah," King said. "Most ants are Baptist or Methodist." That shut Musgrave up.

"Grasshoppers don't bite you," Lobbidy said.

"Which one are you going to be when you grow up, Hughie?" King asked me.

That was harder for me to answer. I always got a lovely lift when a grasshopper bunged and planed and clicketed ahead of me, and there was something quite friendly about an insect that would let you gently squeeze its abdomen and would obligingly spit tobacco juice on the back of your hand. But at the same time a grasshopper had no sense of consequences or obligation. "I wouldn't want to freeze or starve to death in the winter."

"So you're willing to bust your ass working—lugging and pushing and rolling and pulling loads ten thousand times heavier than you are—every day of your life?"

"Better than starving to death when winter comes, isn't it?"

"If you're a worker ant you figure you'll live to see that winter?"

"Well—sure. . . ."

"You won't. What's the life expectancy of an ant—except for the queen?"

"Search me."

"Three months. They're asking you to spend your entire life with no fun at all because of a promise that you will live through a winter you will not see because you're going to die of old age before first snowfall—anyway."

That wasn't the end of it, because we argued about how long a working day the average ant put in and whether or not an ant even slept.

King Motherwell just about cancelled Mr. Mackey out.

As I walked from Government Road towards the Little Souris, the wind and the grasshoppers and the very smell of the prairie itself—grass cured under the August sun, with the subtle menthol of sage—worked nostalgic magic on me. These were the same bannering gophers suddenly stopping up into tent-pegs, the same stilting killdeer dragging her wing ahead of me to lure me away from her young; this was the same sun fierce on my vulnerable and mortal head. Now and as a child I walked out here to ultimate emptiness, and gazed to no sight destination at all. Here was the melodramatic part of the earth's skin that had stained me during my litmus years, fixing my inner and outer perspective, dictating the terms of the fragile identity contract I would have with my self for the rest of my life.

And I was looking down!

When we walked over the prairie we often looked down, for like the badger and the weasel and the skunk and the coyote and the gopher, we were earth creatures. Wild and ham as the prairie was with its droughts and blizzards and sudden seasons, any real beauty was miniature, whether it was foxtail or crocus or pineapple weed or violet or buttercup or buffalo bean, bluebell, or the old man's whiskers.

I moved on through that anticipatory stillness, the wind constant at my cheek and nostrils, stirring my hair, till an old and familiar smell came to me. Wet potter's clay. I reached the river well upstream from the Mental Hospital powerhouse dam, where we had netted suckers in the spring. Here it was more long slough than river, phallic with cat-tails, frogs nudging their snouts and bump eyes through a green gruel of algae. As I walked along the Little Souris, I caught the smell of mint that was almost too perfect and then the perfume musk of wolf willow. I came to the Mental hole. I could not believe that it was this small! No naked boys swam or dived here, nor had they since 1947 when the Rotary Club swimming-pool had been built in town.

At the Mental hole, or further upstream at the CPR role, I was always the first one into and out of the water, crawling up the clay bank, clutching for purchase at willow roots or grass tufts or wild-rose bushes. Under the drip of wet boys' bodies the clay usually baked and cured to hard adobe under the prairie sun, very quickly became a greased slide, and then grey and sucking mud.

The reason I tried always to be first in and first out was that I was small for my age. It was not a matter simply of height and weight; I was *all* small, particularly where it mattered most to me. To avoid public humiliation I was the quickest dresser and undresser of us all. I would come out of the water as infrequently as possible to use the slant diving-board we had put up. I envied the hunchback of Notre Dame.

Until the spring of 1924, the year I was twelve—when most people took me for nine or ten—I was fatalistic. That year the Queen's birthday came on a Saturday and the twenty-fourth of May generally marked our first swim of the season. I started out with Lobbidy Lon Cavanaugh and Austin Musgrave; at the edge of town, just before the Co-op Creamery, we were joined by the Liar and Angus Hannah and Peter Deane-Cooper.

The May afternoon was so warm that after the Fair-grounds and before we'd started to cross Vonneguts' we had all taken off our jackets and sweaters and blouses to feel the sun kind to our mushroom skin. Though there were lots of gophers, no one said, "Let's drown them out instead of having the first swim of the year." It would be wonderful, we told each other; the ice had been out for at least three weeks; a crocus was no longer an event; if you looked hard enough, wild violets could be found. The Liar said he'd heard mead-owlarks two weeks ago and seen four the day before yester-day, and Musgrave said he was lying again. I wanted to believe him.

There was not the usual argument about whether we should head for the CPR hole instead of the Mental hole. Everybody wanted the Mental; I think because we hadn't yet set up our diving-board there. The CPR bridge meant instant immersion through diving and the shock might be brutal. We were just hopeful—not optimistic.

It was reassuring when we got to the Mental hole to find two other boys staring down at the creek. I didn't know them, but Lobbidy did; he said they were from the south side. They decided to go in with us, and we all started undressing.

As usual, I was the first naked; I ran to the bank and threw myself off in a shallow belly-flop. I had made a wrong decision. My plasma and corpuscles must have crystallized instantly.

I managed to stand up, the water a glacial ring around my hips, ice bracelets at both wrists. I lifted my arms clear of the water. By this time the others were yelling from the bank, asking me how it was. Since the shock had snatched my breath, it was difficult for several moments to answer them.

"Just fine!"

Now that I could think as well as breathe and speak, I realized that with water this cold, my penis and scrotum would probably never be seen again.

I turned round, away from the bank, and looking out across the river as though there were something very interesting over there, I lowered my hand into the water. I had not anticipated how difficult it would be, simply by blind touch, to find it down there. Not only must the ice water have shrunk it to nipple size, it had numbed my thumb and forefinger to no feeling at all. Like a robin finally successful on a lawn I did get a hold on the end of it. I pulled it out and held it stretched under water. I relaxed the tension, then pulled again. Even if it had worked, I needn't have bothered, for the others were not noticing anything after they got out. With lips blue, teeth chattering, hands cupping their privates, they crouched shivering and watching Lobbidy and Peter Deane-Cooper getting a cow-flap fire going.

On the way home Musgrave said we'd probably all come down with pneumonia and it would be my fault for suggesting going swimming so early in a year that had a late spring anyway. Actually it had not been a late spring and I had not made the first suggestion at all.

I had started something, however, for when I had my bath that night, I reasoned that if exercise and weightlifting increased the bulk of other muscles it might work for this one. When I towelled myself I stretched it by pulling it to its full length ten times, and just before falling asleep I counted another ten. Before I got out of bed the next morning I exercised it again, but I was interrupted at twenty-three. Melodramatically.

Even though I abandoned that sort of muscle-building for some time, I continued to feel acute guilt and shame. Now I knew what the older boys were talking about when they said you could get "farmers' clap" from "jerking off with a dirty hand" and precisely what the Old Testament and Musgrave meant by "spilling your seed upon the ground." Musgrave was quite knowledgeable and unfortunately credible. I did not care to know that what I had done to myself could make people go blind and send them into the Mental as well. I devoutly hoped it was not too late in my case, and that in time I might be returned to health, if not purity.

I also hoped that no one would ever find out what I had done; I tried not to think about it, for fear that people might guess it from my face. I had some success, for the feelings of shame and uncleanliness began to subside, reviving only when I went out to the Mental hole, especially when Blind Jesus or Horny Harold showed up there with those patients from the Mental who often came to watch us swim. By the end of June I was almost sure I would not become a Mental Hospital citizen.

The last Saturday of the month Peter Deane-Cooper and I went downstream from the others, swimming at first, then floating on our backs, our hands just feathering at our sides, with now and again a kick to keep our feet from sinking and pulling us under. Now and again for Peter, who was a good floater, more often for me because I was mostly bone. There was nothing restful about the way I floated.

About a hundred yards below the Mental hole we both came out because the river had shrunk and shallowed so there. As we walked out, the alkali silt that swallowed our feet to our ankles was astonishing white. One of us, Peter I think, leaned down at the water's edge and dipped up what looked like a handful of wallpaper paste. Peter stirred it in his palm with the tip of his finger, then made a ring around one eye. He looked just like Bill Sykes' pit bull. Peter drew a ring around the other eye and then a moon mouth crescent. Goofy! I wanted my clown face to be a sad one, so I inverted the mouth, whitening my whole upper lip. I also starred my eyes with rays and painted their lids and dragged tear streaks down my cheeks and made a white ball out of my nose, I hoped. I kept turned away from Peter while I did it, then faced him. It must have worked because he laughed that hooty laugh of his till he almost choked.

He turned away from me, and whatever he was doing this time took a lot longer. At first he was bent down and splashing water at his face and rubbing, then he began working at painting his face and his front as well. Finally he moved over to pull up a long cat-tail, strip its leaves, grab it by the center, and lift it high over his head.

He turned to me, savage. Except for the nose and mouth and eye holes he'd left flesh-pink, his face was sheeted white down to a careful cut-off line round the base of his neck. White snakes writhed up the inside and outside of his arms and all over his chest and belly. Thrusting and withdrawing his cat-tail spear he came at me like a Zulu warrior, and he was great!

I turned away from him and I drew a sternum and ribs and tried for a skull face so I would be a skeleton, but halfway through for some reason I changed my mind. Instead I whitened my whole front, except for my crotch, and turned to face Peter. He liked it because he whitened his whole front *and* his prick *and* his balls. I did mine too, and we turned from each other so that we could do each other's back. When we had finished, neither of us laughed any more.

We did not get in the river and wash ourselves off; we let it bake on, and then we started walking over the prairie, watching out for cacti and spear grass. I don't think we spoke to each other all the way back to the Mental hole; we didn't say, "Let's sneak up on the other guys—let's surprise them— maybe scare hell out of Musgrave." We were invoking much more than that, though we did not know what. We simply holy-ghosted our way in a circle out from the river, then in to the Mental hole.

All of them were in the water, except for Lobbidy, who was on the end of the diving-board. As we came up, he turned round and lifted his arms in front of himself, his thumbs hooked together to do a back dive or a back somersault. He managed neither, for he saw us and let out a yell and lost his balance and fell. He came up shouting and pointing us out to the others. We stood on the edge of the bank, looking down at them while they looked up at us with their mouths open.

Peter and I dived in and stayed underwater as long as we could and came up and ducked under again so that when we climbed out the white was all washed off. The others came out too and asked us what we had done and how we had done it. We would not tell them.

That night after I said my "Now I lay me down to sleep"

and just before I dropped off, I wished that King Motherwell had been there to see us.

Looking down from the bank of the Mental hole and remembering, decades later, I wondered why we had done it. I couldn't tell myself. I don't think I can now, though I know it is important to what I've been looking for ever since the dream first came to me.

I knew that I was trying to accomplish the unaccomplishable by searching out here. I walked south-east away from the river, hoping that I would find the abandoned homesteader shack, that it had not been hauled away for use as a granary or torn down for building boards or firewood. I could remember it clearly, halfway between the Mental hole and Brokenshell Grove, faded CPR red, its roof covered with tattered tarpaper and curved like an Indian bow. Inside, under a corner drift of newspapers and rags and other garbage, Peter and I once found an enamel wash-basin, a teapot, a curry comb, a gopher trap that had lost its spade tongue, half a pair of hames, and a little glass boot with criss-cross prints and holes for the laces and a seam up the back from the mold. I recognized it as a Santa Claus boot, once topped by a red-cheeked, white-bearded head and filled with tiny, heart-shaped red candies. Cinnamon usually.

The shack was nowhere out there, and it was no use trying to find the wild-rose bush, for its life expectancy could not possibly have been fifty years, and there must have been all kinds of younger generations by then to confuse me. I needed that shack, and the large rosebush that had hidden the tunnel opening, to find the site of the cave Peter and I had dug in the summer of 1924.

Whatever had made me think that I could be my own archeologist searching the earth of my own past, that I could discover anything out here left behind by our extinct child society? We made no inscriptions, built no monuments, left no arrowheads, chipping-stones, axes, bull-roarers, bows remembering past tension. I should have known I would find nothing that I could hold in my hands to examine and to wonder about and to label.

I did try again before I left. The next day I went to the cemetery.

After standing at the graves of my mother and my father, I went over to the veterans' section of the cemetery to find King Motherwell's. The stone was impressive, a granite cross with a helmet tilted on the top and a rifle with bayonet leaning against it. "Kingsley Spurgeon Motherwell, b. March 14, 1898—d. November 7, 1935." I already knew those dates from the weekly *Gleaner* my mother used to send me. It was my father's paper and in King's obituary he had listed all King's war honors, referring to him as an "oft-decorated hero of the Great War."

I believe I cried then. I did not feel cleansed, simply forlorn.

Now I want to sing of arms and a man.

II

Excepting my father and mother, I suppose that King
Motherwell and William S. Hart were the two people who
marked me most in boyhood. And Peter Deane-Cooper. But
of the three, King's print on me has faded least. Quite
uninvited the memory of him has returned to me again and
again.

I can still summon him easily. At first I cannot see him,
but I can feel his hands making a steady stirrup under my
right foot. I am facing him, my own hands at his shoulders, in
towards the column of his neck. The cords tighten; his hands
lift me up with a powerful upward thrust and I am arching
into a back dive or balling up in a backward somersault into
the muddy Little Souris. Then there comes to me the escargot
taste and smell of the river in the back of my throat and
nostrils.

Still I cannot see him, but I can see his left hand,
fingers fanned with just their tips touching the green felt, the
thumb veeing out from the first knuckle while the cue slides
forward to stop a fraction of an inch short of the white ball,
then again, the butt of the cue held so delicately between
thumb and forefinger, back and forth like a child's toe dragged
under an idling swing.

No one could beat him at snooker or billiards or fluke or
pea pool or the golf game they played a lot. No one could
beat him at anything, in his pool hall, in the trenches in
France, where he won all his medals, or on the ice at the
Arena rink, where he played goal for the Trojans. I can see
him quite clearly, goal skates clumping on wood down the
narrow chute to the ice, with an awkward shoulder swagger

15

because of the wide leg-pads with their coal-scuttle tops. I
can see him reach over and down to unlatch the gate, step
down onto the ice, and shove himself out of all awkwardness
and into a slow and metronomic rock around the rink, the fat
goal-stick held over his shoulder like a rifle. All the others
follow him past the advertisements on the boards: McConkey's
Drugs with its mortar and pestle, Crozier's Men's Wear,
Nightingale's Funeral Home, Firmstone's Department Store,
Riddle's Shoe and Harness, R. W. Cavanaugh's Livery Stables, Marshall's Garage, Co-op Creamery, Isbister Sash and
Door. The Trojan colors were the same as the Boston Bruins':
chocolate and gold socks and sweaters and toques; King
doesn't wear a toque, instead he has a khaki wool Balaclava.
God, how the dirty-playing Melville Millionaires and the
city-arrogant Regina Aces and the Weyburn Beavers of the
Saskatchewan Senior Hockey League must have hated the
very sight of that old Balaclava.

If we didn't see King on the Arena ice in winter we saw
him in the Royal Pool Hall. It was his. Pool halls were not
considered the place for children; indeed I believe there was
some sort of law that said it was criminal to enter one if you
were under sixteen. But it was all right with King if we came
into his pool hall between McConkey's Drugs and Riddle's
Shoe and Harness; most of us went in there a lot, almost as
often as we did into Chan Kai's Blue Bird Cafe, next to my
father's print shop where he published *The Gleaner*. In both
King's and Chan's we could cash in empty pop bottles or use
them as money. King didn't have ice-cream cones or cent
candy the way Chan did, but he did have ginger ale and
Coca-Cola and lemon and lime and orange crush, and Sweet
Marie and Oh Henry! chocolate bars. He would also accept
gopher tails in payment.

Entering King's pool hall was a lot like diving under
water, dim and cool. "They built it before they invented plate
glass," King said. The windows were just like ordinary house
windows with square, small panes; as well, King had the
blinds pulled to keep summer out; the only inside illumina-
tion came from the overhead lights and bounced off the green
felt of four tables down the long, low, submarine cave. The
whole place smelled of Wild Root hair tonic and Tiger Balm,
cigarette and cigar smoke, and was ripe with the chewing-

tobacco smell trumpeted from all the brass spittoons. Fig and molasses.

Once your eyes had adjusted, the first person you saw was usually Leon, working on a customer in one of the chairs to the right, or bent over the sink, or turning away from it with a steaming towel hammocked between his hands. If business were slow he would be sitting in one of his own barber chairs and reading. Usually the Bible. Leon was Holy Roller. He was doctor-pure in the white jacket he wore; he also wore an incredibly black wig that parted right down the middle and arced over his forehead like the wings of a gliding crow. I did not think that a wig, or having to wear one, was very funny; but in Leon's case it did seem ironic, for, being a barber, he should have been able to buy the best wig going. Wholesale. He should also have been able to get decent clippers that could trim your sides and neck less painfully than an attack of fire ants. I was spared them until I was eight, when my father took me in for my first professional haircut; if my mother had had her way I suppose I would have had Buster Brown haircuts and worn a middy until I was seventeen. Eight had been unforgivably late.

Unless he was in the rummy room at the back or on one of his runs over the border into Montana, King sat on a high stool with twisted wire criss-crossing between its legs; it was set behind the glass counter where he collected from the players for games or cigarettes or plugs, and now and again a cigar out of the boxes with dark Latin ladies on their lids. There were things below the counter-top that a child could buy: staghorn jack-knives, mouth organs, and clay pipes that cost only a cent and were good for blowing bubbles, though their stems robbed your lips and tongue, your whole mouth, of all saliva. Unpleasantly. They could be smoked, once charged with dried Virginia-creeper leaves or corn tassels or tea. When you were young, Macdonald fine-cut, or Old Chum when you were older. Except for their shorter stems these clay pipes were like the one being smoked in the Old Chum poster by the jolly old English squire in his white wig and square glasses, sitting with his plump, buttoned belly on his spread knees in the sun before an English pub. The stem on his clay pipe was gracefully curved and at least four feet long. On the wall above and behind King there was a constellation of lacrosse and baseball and hockey team pictures, with fellows in their uniforms kneeling and sitting and standing. You could find King in every one of them. Also Eddie Crozier. But not in uniform; he was just the manager of the Trojans.

Just under the ceiling of pressed-tin squares with acanthus leaves and rosettes, a shelf ran almost the whole length of that side of the pool hall. King had probably put it up there himself with angled metal brackets for the life-size ducks and geese with their necks bolt upright or snaked out in the feeding position. King had carved them all.

He seemed to carve them mostly during the winter months, finding them again in blocks of pine after they'd flown south. Cedar wouldn't do, he said, because it wouldn't take and hold the detail the way pine would, and besides pine was nicer to work with, more satisfying, the way it seemed to declare itself when carved.

When he carved he wore a celluloid visor so that the upper half of his face was shaded green and when he started out he would have his carving arm at full length out from himself, the block down at his thighs as he began to impose the rough beginnings of form. At the last he would have it clutched up to his chest, the knife handle almost swallowed in his hand, its tip digging and etching the feather detail.

"Pintail, this one." He held it out over the counter towards Lobbidy and me one time. "Pointy ass—wings set so far back on them compared to a mallard. Almost like they got no ass at all. Easy to tell pintails in the air. Out of the bigger ones. Any idiot can tell a teal or a butterball because they're so small."

He carved all the ducks there were: canvasbacks, spoonbills, buffleheads, mergansers, and even wood ducks, though there weren't any of those ever in our part of the world. He once showed me a dear little blue-winged teal he had just painted. "Just your size, Hughie. I'll carve you one some day." I would have preferred a harlequin or a Canada honker. I also coveted the pictures of well-bred dogs playing poker, the gentlemanly collie, the pert, card-cheating terrier, the cynical pit bull. The sad but dignified Saint Bernard, with pince-nez glasses, looked exactly like Judge Hannah. For that matter, the terrier looked a lot like Eddie Crozier.

I cannot recall ever hearing King truly blasphemous or obscene. Once when Peter and I were in the pool hall, Hilton Fraser missed an easy eight ball on the third table and started cursing. Among other things, he said there was no way he could get those "cock-suckers" into pockets that were "mean, skinny little cunts!" King didn't even go round the end of the counter. He bunged up off his high stool and over, grabbed Hilton by the seat of his pants and the back of his neck, and pranced him down the hall and out the front door. He told Peter and me to just finish up our pop and get out.

Out on the street after, Peter said the pockets on all four tables were micrometer-measured to professional size and that Hilton Fraser was a foul-mouthed prick anyway. It was ironic that King should be so careful of his own language and that of his players in front of kids when most of us talked dirty all the time. In his own way Austin Musgrave was the worst; he could talk dirty without using any dirty words—just ones out of the Bible.

We also saw King a lot out at the Mental hole, for like most heroes he was a magnificent swimmer; from the twenty-fourth of May to late fall he joined us often out at the Mental hole, driving his seven-passenger McLaughlin right over the bald prairie to the Little Souris. The Judge Hannahs had a seven-passenger McLaughlin too, but it wasn't maroon with yellow-spoked wheels, nor did it have the bullet-shaped little vases always filled with wild flowers King picked: crocuses in early spring, buffalo beans, brown-eyed susans, bluebells, and tiger lilies and goldenrod later on. On the two front doors he had his monogram in gold: K.S.M.

Out at the Mental hole, King went through the same ritual every time: took off his coat and sleeveless sweater and shirt, stepped out of his bell-bottom trousers and underwear, folded them and placed them on the front seat of his car, then threw himself off the bank into a long and thrusting dive to duck and roll and make the moon rise. He would come up facing most of us, lower his head so the water line reached just under his nose, then expel his breath in short, bubbling blasts—silly sounds just like angry elephant squeals. Right away he would start to swim upstream, doing the side stroke, his left arm pulling down and along his side, the other thrown high and forward over-arm again and again with the wrist and

hand loose and sloppy, yet synchronized with a scissors kick
that drove him ahead in powerful surges. From the side of his
face a small wave veed right out to either bank; you knew he
could keep it up forever; it was as though he intended
swimming all the way to the Souris and all the way to the Red
and all the way to the Saskatchewan and Hudson Bay and
maybe across the Atlantic to England. He could have swum
the Hellespont. Easily. But only if he felt like it.

At one time or another most of us tried to follow him
upstream—unsuccessfully. We all ran out of steam, the way
side stroke took it out of you and you had to roll over onto
your back to rest your arms and legs and get your wind back
and then each time you turned over, King would be further
away until you couldn't even see him any more and you
climbed out onto the bank and your legs and your whole
body felt just like lead.

After three or four tries that summer, I did make it, in
early August when the river was low and the current almost
dead. I simply stayed on my back, mainly shoving with my
hands at my sides and kicking just enough to keep my body
level. I didn't even know where I was till I finally rolled over
to discover I was just downstream from the CPR bridge, a
good mile above the Mental hole. It wasn't really a river here
but a wide and shallow slough, its edges speared with bulrushes.
I lowered my feet and instead of just touching with the tips of
my toes, I could stand, the muddy bottom squelching up
between my toes. I looked upstream and there was King
under the CPR bridge. He was all covered with white foam.

I was a little worried; he hadn't invited me to follow him.
He was lathering up his hair and then under his arms and
then his crotch. He turned and he saw me.

"Hi."

"King."

"Wondered when you'd make it."

I didn't know he'd known I had swum after him those
other times.

He reached out and tucked a bar of yellow laundry soap
up into the corner where the last trestle support was, and I
knew then that he always kept a bar of soap up there and
when this one had thinned down he'd replace it with a fresh
one. I also knew that this must be what he did every time he

came swimming, which would make him just about the cleanest person in our district. In spring and summer and fall anyway.

"Easier going back—*down*stream."

He dived in and I could see the wide circle he swam under water to rinse himself off, suds and bubbles rising and betraying him. When he came up, his hair was parted right down the middle and hung down in two black wings, the tips at the corners of his jaw.

"Hey! You look just like Colleen Moore!"

He got me right in the chest; I should have noticed his cheeks ballooned out before he squirted me. He threw his head back and his wet hair flopped and he smoothed it down with his hands and he didn't look like Colleen Moore with her Dutch bob, but like Rudolph Valentino with his plastered pompadour and long sideburns.

He came out of the water and for a moment he was turned away from me while he reached up to the trestle again; his head tilted and held, and then he put the brown bottle back up with the soap. I guess he replaced that, too, whenever it ran out.

We went up on the bridge and sat with our legs hung over to dry off and the smell that came from him in the hot sun was both caustic and sweet: laundry soap and whiskey. Now I could get a good look at the serpent. Vein blue and faint rust-pink and green it came out of the black bush of his pubic hair; scaled and about half as thick as my wrist, it coiled around his belly button and then up under his left nipple and across his chest to loop round his right nipple. The flat head with its almond eyes and forked tongue was cradled in the hollow of his throat just over his sternum.

"Don't you ever be stupid enough to get yourself tattooed."

I didn't realize it had been obvious to him that I was staring at his snake there.

"Understand!"

I said sure I did and I promised him I wouldn't. He didn't have to warn me. The Liar maybe. The Liar was already tattooing himself all the time by licking the end of his indelible pencil and then drawing on the backs of his hands and his forearms. The Liar could hardly wait to grow up and get to a tattoo parlor.

"I got drunk one leave."

"Did it hurt much?"

"Of course. Punch and prick you with a needle—blue dye and green and yellow—red and orange, but when that's all mixed with your own blood it doesn't show—scab forms over the whole thing—I had to sleep on my back over a week. Then the scab sloughs off and there it is."

He stood up.

"Rest of your life. Don't ever do anything you can't undo."

"Better tell the Liar that."

"Seemed like a good idea at the time." He laughed. "Another serpent crawling out of the buffalo-berry bush in the Garden of Eden." Then right away his face got serious. "Let's go." He started down off the bridge. "Not just tattoos either."

Swimming back he must have slowed down deliberately for me because we stayed side by side halfway to the Mental hole, then he suggested we get out and rest for a few minutes. We did, but as soon as we sat down on the bank, he got up and walked over to a big clump of rosebush and bent over it. When he came back the fruity smell of the whiskey was much stronger.

We didn't say anything for a while, just sat, King with his elbows on his knees and his arms hanging loose. The smell of sage was strong and there must have been mint near by; it was too early yet for wolf willow.

"You know—there aren't just ten commandments," King said. "They must have over a hundred of them by now. Thou shalt not smoke. Thou shalt not drink. Thou shalt not wear rouge or lipstick or open galoshes or yellow slicker raincoats. Thou shalt not have a cootie-catcher hairdo. Thou shalt not fart. Hell—more like a thousand, and the funny thing is they didn't even need them—all they needed was the one commandment."

"What one?"

"Thou shalt not have fun. Covers nearly everything—doesn't it? Not official—doesn't say in the Bible Moses went up on that mountain and there was a bolt of lightning and he found *eleven* graven tablets and there it was on that eleventh one—in Hebrew—ancient Hebrew—thou shalt not have fun! I had my way he would have found a twelfth tablet up there while he was at it!"

"What twelfth?"

"*My* commandment! My own! There has been too much thou-shalt-notting going on all through all the centuries of man and all of this thou-shalt-notting has got to stop. Kingsley Spurgeon Motherwell's commandment is: 'Thou shalt not—shalt not.' *I* shalt not—that's all right—but no more of this 'Thou shalt not. Thou shalt not—*thou* shalt not.'"

It didn't seem so strange for King to talk that way; he often did, perhaps because his father had been a Methodist minister, one of the early missionaries on Assiniboine and Salteaux reserves in Manitoba and Saskatchewan. King's mother died in Fort Qu'Appelle. That was in 1900 when King was two. He was twelve when his father took over Grace Methodist in our town. Right at the beginning of the war King lied about his age and joined up. He had just reached sixteen, barely three years older than I was that summer of 1924. They needed him over there in the war.

It probably didn't surprise anyone in our district that they made him a sniper right away. He must have handled a twenty-two rifle before he was eight, wandering over the prairie to lie flat out on his stomach with the rifle butt snugged into his shoulder, squeezing the trigger slow on gophers he got in his peep sights. The flat *whap* of the twenty-two must have been an early familiar for him, and the *thuck* as the bullet hit, and the firecracker smell that lingered after.

They gave him all kinds of medals before the war was finished and he made it back home. Alive and without a scratch. "I'm lucky and I got strong medicine," I heard King say several times.

His father had died in the 1918 flu epidemic. I don't think King ever looked upon that as a terribly tragic event.

For three years or so he worked in the Mental as an attendant, and it was during his last year out there that Bill the Sheepherder made his first escape, one of many he would make during the next five years. Bill was a bachelor and like King a war veteran. Before he was committed he had run sheep on nearly three sections of land in the Manyberries district along the Montana border. That is mostly short grass and badlands country, which might explain why Bill, before and after the war, was into sheep instead of cattle. He did not have a brilliant war record the way King did, but by the time he had escaped five times from the Mental he was almost as famous as Prime Minister William Lyon Mackenzie King or Lon Chaney in our district.

In his first escape he managed to stay one jump ahead of the Mounties for a week, but he did leave a trail of farmhouse raids and break-ins for food and, as it turned out, weapons. The trail led right to the Manyberries badlands country, where the police ran him to ground in his own place. There he took pot-shots at farmers passing by in buggies, Model-T's, grain wagons. From their reports the police figured he had a Springfield, a thirty-thirty, a twenty-two, and a ten-gauge goose gun. He held off most of the RCMP detachment and the Manyberries district population for a day, a night, and most of the following morning.

King was there and at noon he told Inspector Kydd that he knew Bill pretty well from the Mental, that Bill knew he was a fellow veteran and not a Mounted Policeman, and if Constable Barney Elderfield tried to walk in as they were planning, Bill would probably drop him in his tracks. According to the story my father did for the *Leader* and his own weekly, King suggested they let him talk to Bill. Inspector Kydd agreed and King began to call out to Bill. He also began to walk towards the house through the spring rain. He kept right on going, just as though he were paying Bill a visit, until he judged he was inside Bill's sight-line, then ducked low and ran around the corner to the side door.

He burst in just as Bill came in the back door. Both of them made it at the same time to the cot under one of the windows, with its cargo of guns and ammunition. It was a touch-and-go struggle with Bill before King got him under control. "I was just lucky," he said. "I had no way of knowing Bill had held out as long as he could without a trip to the backhouse. Every step I took to the front of that house, I figured it would be my last one. Lucky for me he had diarrhea!"

It was that fall King stopped working out at the Mental to take over the pool hall. Musgrave told me King didn't make enough money out at the Mental to buy the pool hall, or out of the pool hall to buy a seven-passenger McLaughlin touring car. I said what did he make it out of then, and

Musgrave said out of the rummy room at the back of the pool hall, and out of what he sold in there by the shot glass, and out of all the runs he made over the border, taking hummocks and coyote- and badger-holes at full throttle with lights out and all the sacks and cases of bottles clinking. Musgrave had a nasty way of knowing all about what other people did. Especially if it was something they weren't supposed to be doing. He was extremely well informed, simply by listening to his parents, I suspected.

King still carried a twenty-two with him in his McLaughlin. Always. He kept it cradled across the two little jump-seats that folded up into slots in the back of the front seat, along with a thirty-ought-thirty and a lovely double-barrel twelve-gauge Boswell with an Italian walnut stock; it had pheasants and bird dogs exquisitely etched too in silver. His gold monogram was on the shotgun too. He was always touching off weasels and jack-rabbits, badgers and coyotes, prairie chicken in fall, and out at Yellow Grass and Brokenshell sloughs, ducks and Canada honkers.

King must be my only ghost. He has haunted me for over half a century, but not, I hope, for the usual haunt reasons he once explained to Peter Deane-Cooper and me.

"Why do you think they close the eyes of the dead just as quick as they can?" he once said to us. I hadn't even known they did that. "Make them look like they are just sleeping. Now—why do they want them to seem to be *not* dead? Because they can't stand those dead eyes staring at them—accusing them."

"What of?"

"Being alive. Being dead is not worth a damn, so the dead are mad at the living because the living are still living and the dead are dead. They envy us. Happy hunting grounds, Paradise—Heaven *or* Hell—life after death is just one big load of elderly bullshit! So just don't you eat that, Elmer. Ghosts, well there's some room for doubt there. If there are ghosts I'll tell you something. There aren't any kind ones— nor helpful—they're out to make trouble for us living lucky ones. Egyptians knew that, that's why they doubled up the knees of their dead and cinched them tight, right away before rigor mortis set in. Just you look out for ghosts. Especially mine. I will make the meanest ghost in town! I'll haunt everybody. Well, no, not everybody."

"Not me," Peter said.

"Or me," I said.

"Maybe not. There is one batch of humans I know I wouldn't have it in for—those poor bastards out at the Mental!"

That August day, after King and I walked the last half of the way back to the Mental hole, we found all the others had left. We dressed and he said to climb in and he'd give me a ride back to town. But before we got there he turned into the Fairgrounds and out onto the race track and then opened the McLaughlin right out, and the wind took my hair and pumped out my blouse and when I held my mouth half opened, it filled out my cheeks just like a balloon.

After five times around, King spread his legs and let me sit between them and steer the car and shove up the gas as far as I wanted; I didn't shove it very far up. We didn't leave right away because King reached down in the pocket in his door and brought out a flask and then just sat there.

I have never ever known anyone who made me laugh as much as King did—not clown laugh-making or boob laugh-making the way the Liar always tried to do. Unsuccessfully. King would tell you that something was enough to give a gopher's ass the heartburn, that H. B. Critchley, who managed the Home Bank, was tighter than a cow's ass in fly time and wouldn't pay a dime to see a piss ant eat a bale of hay. He said once that Charlie Riddle was so stubborn if he were to drown they'd have to look for his body upstream. King did not seem to approve of too many adults.

But this time in the car he wasn't talking all that funny; it was one of the few times I ever heard him talk about the war.

"You believe what they said Cecil Rhodes said—on his deathbed?"

"I got no idea what they said he said."

"'So much to do—so little time.' He rared up on his deathbed and those were his last words. 'So much to do—so little time.' You believe he said that?"

"If they said he said it—maybe he said it."

"He didn't."

"How do you know he didn't?"

"I been there."

"Cecil Rhodes' deathbed!"

"Other ones. My partner, Merv, when he got it—I was right beside him. Shell hole, trench mortar—right in the belly. You could see his intestines just like a ball of garter-snakes all wove together in the spring. You think he lifted up onto his elbow and he said, 'So much to do—so little time'? Famous last words said by Corporal Mervin Herbig, lineman for Saskatchewan Telephone Company out of Moose Jaw. You believe that's what he said with his last dying breath? Nope. Oh, sure, he did *try* to lift up on one elbow, but he didn't have the strength left to do that and keep all his guts in. I heard him—plain as day—he said, 'Aw horse shit!'"

I believed that.

"When people are dying they haven't got time to get off good last words—unless maybe they decided ahead of time what they were going to say for their famous last words. They should. They owe it to the rest of the world. When famous people are dying there's always a lot of people hanging around waiting to hear what their famous last words will be—pencil and paper all ready to take it down—or make it up. Of all people you'd think Queen Victoria would have been ready, but she wasn't. She didn't look up to all those ladies-in-waiting round her bed and say, 'We are not amused.' Oh, she tried to all right but her teeth were in a glass on the night-stand by the bed, so she just had to settle for a fart—one last long whispery old-age royal fart."

"You decided what yours are going to be?"

"Mmm-hmh."

"What?"

"I get the chance—I'll say: 'Time to piss on the fire and call the dog.'"

He started up the McLaughlin. "Ought to do it."

He let me out at home.

Just before I went to sleep that night I got to thinking about the direction he always drove from whenever he came out to the Mental hole. He never came from the east, the town side. It was always from the west. The Mental was to the north; the CPR bridge was to the south. To the west was Brokenshell Grove, but before that were the three little cottages with bonnet roofs. That meant that King must have driven to the Mental hole from Sadie Rossdance's before he dived in and swam upstream and soaped himself with Sunlight laundry soap under the CPR bridge. Every time.

I hoped then that he would not haunt me for envy; I hope now that he has haunted me for over half a century—only for love.

III

A Small and sardonic man, my father brought out a weekly, *The Gleaner*, in what he called "the print shop" and my mother called "the newspaper office." On the masthead of *The Gleaner*, it said "WE COVER THE PRAIRIES." I often heard my father add, "But I'm not saying with what." Much of the time he aimed his irony at himself, but he still had lots left over for others. "You're just like him," my mother frequently said to me. In spite of loving us both, I don't think she found either of us easy to live with.

Besides his small stature, I seemed to have inherited my father's pulmonary system; like him I suffered from recurring bouts of bronchitis. He had a chronic cough which I did not have, so it was probably true that it could have been caused, as my mother told him often enough, by all the pipes and cigars he smoked. I'm not sure whether my mother really believed this, for it did not explain why she nearly panicked every time I snuffed or sneezed. I never did hear her mention tuberculosis, a most embarrassing disease, with a degree of mortification comparable to what might be caused today by public knowledge of congenital syphilis in your family. She felt that Canadians did not go in for dying of "galloping consumption" nearly so much as the British and Indians did. T.B. had no right to infect her husband or her son. She was quite stubborn about that; when my father died at fifty-seven in the fall of 1936 and I came home from Toronto, where I was doing post-graduate work, my mother said it had been pneumonia. Dr. Sinclair told me sadly that for five years he had been unable to persuade my father to go into the San at Fort Qu'Appelle.

I think my earliest memory of my father is a tactile one, the feel of his hand under my chin as he tilted my face up to himself and told me to open my eyes wide so he wouldn't miss with the medicinal drops for my pink-eye. I must have been two or three then, and not much longer after that there was the slightly hoarse sound of his voice reading me *Grimm's Fairy Tales, Jason and the Golden Fleece, The Water Babies, Mrs. Wiggs of the Cabbage Patch*. He also read me *Black Beauty*, at the end of which he confided to me that he found Black Beauty to be a self-pitying whiner. I disagreed.

He taught me to read the year I was four, by phonically sounding words from the *Regina Leader* and *The Gleaner*, and I remember his delight when I was successful with Tutankhamen. He took me with him down to the shop the next morning, and got me to read the whole lead from the newspaper for anyone who dropped in. I remember that one of the men was Judge Hannah, Angus's father. At least my dad didn't make me memorize all of "Robert Bruce and the Spider" and wear a kilt and a bonnet with a turkey feather in it to recite in, and to wear to Knox Presbyterian Sunday School, where Mrs. Judge Hannah taught us. It could have been Angus's mother who got him to recite in kilts.

Like Judge Hannah, my father was an unrepentant Conservative in the Liberal West. He spoke often of Sir John A. Macdonald, the founding father of Canadian Confederation, and of Sir Robert Borden. He had gone to school in Ontario with Arthur Meighen, leader of the Conservative party, and there was a picture of him in our music room at the end of the row made up by Handel, Bach, Beethoven, Brahms, Liszt, Mozart. My mother sang alto in the Knox Presbyterian choir and Meighen's picture had been a wedding present, though it hadn't been hung until Mr. Meighen came west and to our house for dinner.

We all went into the music room after dinner so my mother could sing "Hanging Apples on the Lilac Tree," and Mr. Meighen said he was glad to see that they still had his picture hung up there, and I said they'd found it in the billiard-room closet the night before, and the nail they'd used instead of a proper picture hook had knocked out a big chunk of plaster, but the hole was covered up by the picture anyway. Then my mother played the upright-grand Heintzman and sang "Believe Me If All Those Endearing Young Charms," which generally made me cry.

My father despised William Lyon Mackenzie King and in the spring of 1922 did not print a word about the Prime Minister's visit to Sir Walter Raleigh School. When my father came home from the shop that evening he listened as I told him about Mr. King's white-piped vest, about how Angus Hannah had recited "Robert Bruce and the Spider," and the Fours and Fives from Miss Coldtart's room, in their Brownie and Cub uniforms, had done their marching and Union Jack drill with arms swinging and knees high and without a hitch, and then the Prime Minister had given a speech and presented the IODE war pictures, one for each classroom and the Principal's office. I saw Mr. Mackey's painting quite a few times before I was through with Sir Walter Raleigh School. *Somewhere With a Veterinary Unit in France*, it showed a number of soldiers with bloody bandages around their heads next to a field gun, with a lot of swollen-bellied, dead horses lying around.

I did not tell my father that I had been a little disappointed when I first heard Mr. King speak; it didn't seem right to me that a Prime Minister should have such a thin, dull voice. When I had finished, my father said, "An elementary school is no place for covert pedophiliacs."

My mother did not get angry with him, but I suspect it was because she didn't know what a pedophiliac was. I was smart enough not to ask him. The closest I could find in the Webster's International in his den was "pedologist" and I didn't think my father would go to the trouble of calling our Prime Minister either a specialist in child study or a soil scientist.

My father had an unwilling admiration for Sir Wilfrid Laurier. "Two strikes against him—French *and* Liberal. Better to be seduced by Laurier's silver tongue than slapped unconscious by that pig's bladder of King's!" I think that if Sir Wilfrid Laurier had ever made a campaign visit to Sir Walter Raleigh, my father might have covered it with a story in *The Gleaner*, and not just as an item in his "Newsy Notes From Round About" column next to "Diseases of Cattle, Horses, Swine, and Poultry"; Laurier would have made it to the front page.

That was *their* world; by the summer of 1924 it was quite a separate one from ours, and during that summer I drew further from my father and much closer to King Motherwell. It was not just that I was spending more time with King till school started in September, but that King had always moved through our world. He was both boy and adult. In winter he coached us in the Arena at hockey, and though my father had taught me to skate when I was very young, he no longer joined us on the frozen Little Souris out at the Mental hole. King did often. And I dropped into the Royal Pool Hall much more than I did into my father's shop. My father never swam with us in the river. He could not swim. I was much more careful with my language around my father than I was with King, and I think he was more careful about his with me than with his friends. We were both of us more careful with my mother.

That summer of 1924 we dug two caves, or rather, *started* one and finished one. Lobbidy Lon Cavanaugh and the Liar and Angus .Hannah and Peter Deane-Cooper and Austin Musgrave and I began one in Austin's back yard. Just Peter Deane-Cooper and I dug the second one in Muhlbiers' sheep pasture between the Mental hole and Brokenshell Grove, our own secret one.

The summer of 1924 was unusually hot and dry with no rain through most of May and June so that we spent a great deal of time swimming out at the Mental hole or the CPR hole in the Little Souris, or lying under somebody's caragana. The day we began the first cave, we had all been in the shade of Musgraves' hedge, wondering whether we should go out to the Mental hole to swim, or to the building site of the new Co-op Creamery to find tar, or north of town to drown out gophers, or over to the sash-and-door factory for scrap lumber to build stilts or to build kites or to build arrow guns, or to the blacksmith shop for horseshoe nails. Someone said it would be fun to dig a cave which would be lovely cool. Austin said we could do it in his back yard and Lobbidy said he had boards so we ought to build it in his yard so we wouldn't have to haul the boards over to Musgraves' yard, and Musgrave said he couldn't leave because his grampa might wake up from his afternoon nap and go out and get lost and he had promised his mother he wouldn't let that happen again, so we'd better dig the cave in his back yard, and if we pitched in right away we'd have the cave finished before his grampa woke up. We agreed to that.

Musgrave's house was four blocks south of our house on Sixth Street; the Liar and Angus Hannah lived closer to me, but I suppose I saw more of Musgrave than I did of them or any other boy in town. This was not my choice. I can still see Musgrave's very freckled face snarling into the sun in birthday-party and school-class photos, though not in my Sunday-school picnic pictures, for the Musgraves were Baptist. We were Presbyterian. Peter Deane-Cooper was Anglican. Lobbidy Lon was Catholic. I think the Liar was Methodist.

Musgrave could make me feel warm and liked. He did this by skilfully creating confidentiality, then bonding me by revealing to me how dirty and mean all the other fellows really were, by telling me what they were saying about me behind my back and what they planned to do to me. He once told me, for instance, that Peter Deane-Cooper had got a four-foot length of half-inch galvanized pipe from behind Nickerson's Plumbing and Heating, and that Peter intended to hide in Hannah's caragana, then stick the pipe into the spokes of my bike's front wheel when I rode by. Musgrave would then fill the sick void within me with protestations of undying friendship and promises that from now on he would never play with anybody but me and that I must play with nobody else but him and that he would help me get even with the others. He would not make all that strong an ally, because he couldn't put anybody down and must have known that, for he never *tried* to put anyone down. Male. He ran. He must have been the fastest runner in town or in Saskatchewan or in Canada or in North America. For his age. Musgrave's totem would have to be the wildebeest. Even more fitting, the coyote.

He had a grampa, his mother's father, a tall, ropy octogenarian with buttermilk-blue eyes and the sad and equine face of William S. Hart. I do not know of any film cowboys who came before William S. Hart; he actually pre-dated the cowboy hat itself, later to be worn by Ken Maynard and Hoot Gibson and Tom Mix. William S. Hart's hat was either Boy Scout or RCMP issue, with leather thongs knotted under his chin. We never were given a close shot of William

S. Hart's face next to his horse's; you could not have told it from his horse's. Same with Austin's grampa, if he were near a horse.

Musgrave's after-fours and Saturdays were often ruined by his grampa; Sundays had already been damaged for all of us by adults. Musgrave's grampa was always getting lost. He would get out of the house and the yard and down the street in his Boy Scout hat, with his cane and with a lumpy knapsack between his shoulder-blades, and Musgrave would have to go all over town, knocking on strange doors and asking people if they'd seen anything of his grampa who had got lost again. That did not work if the old man had made it out onto the prairie beyond the town limits.

Musgrave's grampa seemed to have led a most interesting life; he said he had been imprisoned in Fort Garry by Louis Riel when the Red River Rebellion started, that he was a close friend of Scott, whom Riel executed in 1869. In the Saskatchewan Rebellion, when Louis came back from Montana to lead the half-breeds again, Musgrave's grampa was the first man out of Colonel Boulton's Rangers to set foot in Batoche after it fell. He sat on the jury that condemned Louis Riel to hang in 1885. By using simple arithmetic and his age, you knew he could have done all these things, and I believed him till Musgrave said his grampa was an historical liar. I still thought he was interesting.

No one was ever able to get behind the old man: he always sat in a corner with the two walls meeting behind his back; this was so in the Musgrave house or anywhere else. Musgrave's mother had to cut her father's hair and shave him because he refused to sit in Leon's barber chair, his back unprotected in the Royal Pool Hall. If he met someone on the street and stopped to talk, he must have felt vulnerable, for he would always circle uneasily until he had a building wall or a hedge or a fence at his back. Sometimes he would have to settle just for a telephone pole.

He had a very sensible reason for this: "They're coming to get me one day!" It was never quite clear to me who was coming to get him one day, though I had my suspicions. Whoever it was pretty nearly had to be a half-breed and a close relative or friend of Louis Riel.

I sincerely believed that someone was after him; nobody

would have spent as much time as he did out in the Musgrave
privy, if someone weren't coming to get him one day. From
the May meadowlark when the sun had got high and strong to
all harvest he spent more time out there, with four walls
closing safe around him, than he did in the house. I can
hardly recall a visit to Musgraves' that there wasn't blue
smoke breathing from the diamond cut-out in their backhouse
door. We had inside plumbing.

Another thing about Musgrave's grampa: he had saliva
trouble. It was as though his glands manufactured it perpetu-
ally so that he had to keep gathering it and gathering it until
his mouth had a full cargo of it, then he would shake his head
violently from side to side and spit. He did this about every
thirty seconds. In the house there were spittoons for him,
which Musgrave had to empty every other day. Whenever
you saw Austin's grampa going down Sixth Street his expecto-
ration rate was about once to every hundred paces and always
on alternating sides. Whoever was coming to get him one day
would simply have to follow the saliva trail he left.

The summer of 1924 was a year after Peter Deane-
Cooper had migrated to Canada with his family from England.
Like me he was an only child. His father was an engineer
with the company doing coal strip-mining along the Montana
border. All through his first Canadian winter, even in forty-
below weather, Peter's mother kept him wearing short English stove-pipe pants, with knee socks that had a length of
ribbon hanging down from them just like bookmarkers. Peter
had blue knees all that winter.

To make our cave we all carried boards over from Lobbidy's,
went home for our own round-nosed shovel or spade or pick
or garden fork or bar. Like the gopher and the coyote, the
badger and the weasel, we were all digging animals; with the
prairie tree situation we pretty well had no choice. Our
cave-digging technique never varied: first the sod squares
had to be cut out with a spade, then carefully laid aside so
that they could be placed back over the cave roof later in
exactly the same relationship they'd initially had to each
other. After the cave had been dug deep enough, boards
would be laid across the excavation, the spoil spread out over
the boards and tramped down, the sods replaced. The result
would be only a slight earth swelling. We hoped. As well we

would dig a narrow trench, cover it with short boards, an
camouflage the resulting tunnel in the same way we had don
the cave itself. Nowhere in *A Thousand Things a Boy Ca
Do* is this cave-digging method mentioned.

Shovel and spade and fork plunged easily through th
eighteen inches of topsoil in Musgraves' back yard, but whe
we got down to the hardpan the clay was heart- and back
breaking. Rock hard, in this dry year, it loosened unde
pick and bar in reluctant sugar-lumps. Stinging with sweat
we rested often, reclining at the edge of our shallow excava
tion.

"If a fellow only had a fresno and a team, he could reall
scoop her out." That was Lobbidy.

"If a fellow could soak her good," the Liar said, "run he
full of water—soften her up . . ."

"Easy digging then," Angus said.

"Yeah!" I said.

"If a fellow could only blow her out," the Liar said.

"How?" I said.

"Search me," Lobbidy said.

"Stumping-powder—dynamite." That was the Liar again

"It's our yard."

"Oh yes—indeed—dynamite." Peter always spoke with
that polite English accent that English people always have. I
southern Saskatchewan they certainly do.

"Whump an' she'd blow our cave for us," the Liar said.

"It's not your yard!"

"She sure would," Lobbidy said.

"Only place I know—where they got dynamite—CPI
sheds," the Liar said.

"We can't go swiping dynamite," Angus said.

"I tell you—it's our back yard!"

"I can get you dynamite." Up until Peter said that I hac
been thinking how stupid Musgrave was to keep right on
saying it was his back yard. He ought to know that dynamite
simply did not belong in our world, that it was quite *imagi
nary* dynamite we had been tossing around in conversation
But now I knew that Deane-Cooper meant *real* dynamite
and I felt sick.

"We can't go swiping dynamite." Angus must have fel
sick too; he knew just as well as I did that if Peter Deane
Cooper said he could get you dynamite, he not only *could* ge

you dynamite, you could not *stop* him from getting you dynamite.

"We don't know a thing about handling dynamite," I said.

"I do."

"I think it's a great idea!" The Liar would think that! "Why not?"

"We might wake up Musgrave's grampa." Somehow, even as I said that, I knew there must be a better reason for us not to set off dynamite in Musgraves' back yard.

"Had most of his nap by now—hasn't he?" Peter got up. He said to Austin, "Are you frightened?"

"Uh—no." Musgrave was lying. "Won't it be dangerous?"

"No."

"Why won't it be?" I said.

"In the first place—our cave location. There's nothing dangerously near it at all. Over sixty yards from the back porch." That was true. Our cave site was about halfway between the Musgrave house and the Musgrave backhouse, beyond which there was open prairie. To the right and a good hundred feet away was a pile of wood chunks, perhaps four cords of them. Not stacked. Just in a heap. Almost the same distance on the other side were two clothes-line poles. "In the second place," Peter was saying, "I'm very good with dynamite. I helped my father—in the old country."

"We can't go swiping dynamite," Angus said.

"My father has a whole case of sixty percent in the garage. You—Lobbidy—have them do the hole."

"I'll come with you," the Liar said, the son of a bitch!

"What hole?" Lobbidy said.

"For the dynamite—with the bar—straight down about four foot, I should say."

"I'll come with you."

"Whole goddam case?" Lobbidy said.

"Dead centre—the hole." Peter and the Liar were already heading for the Deane-Cooper garage.

"Is he bringing back a whole case?" Angus's face was worried.

"Goddam the Liar!" Lobbidy said.

I agreed with him. If the Liar hadn't been so enthusiastic about the dynamite, maybe Peter wouldn't have insisted we blow our cave.

"Anything happens it's his fault just as much as Peter's."
Musgrave always knew whose fault everything was.

We never called Russell Matheson the Liar to his face.
He lied a great deal. There was nothing *useful* about his lies;
he was a pure liar. Strangler Lewis, he said, was his uncle.
On his mother's side. The Minister of Agriculture, Federal,
was his uncle too. Also by marriage. Another uncle had
invented the Eskimo pie. He had an older sister, much older,
who had grown up and left the Matheson family to be a
missionary in India. Her name was Vera and she seemed
quite important to the Liar, for the way he always said her
name made me think of Rogers' Golden Corn Syrup pouring.
Vera was brilliant. Vera possessed a brain three times larger
than your average human brain, and indeed scientists in
Germany had already made arrangements to get her brain for
study purposes. After she died. I never ever saw the Liar's
sister, Vera, but if she ever came home on sabbatical from the
mission fields of India, I knew I'd sure as hell recognize her
even at a long distance, with that great big, puffed-up head
three times larger than normal.

I preferred the Liar to Musgrave; if the Liar said something mean about you, it didn't damage you, because everybody knew that nine times out of ten he was lying. He always
smelled like sheep because he had eczema and the ointment
for it must have had a lanolin base. The very fact that he
never said his eczema ointment was made out of sheep would
lead a person to believe that was a true explanation of why he
always smelled like a sheep.

With the Liar it was hard to tell whether he even had an
older sister named Vera.

The hole went down rather slowly until Peter and the
Liar returned with the dynamite. Three sticks. Peter just
tossed them on the ground and took over authority. He did
twice his share of punching down the dynamite hole, stopping only to estimate how much further we had left to go
down. When it suited him, he dropped two of the sticks
down, one on top of the other. There was no tenderness in
the way he handled that dynamite. Besides the three sticks
he had brought back a length of fuse and a copper tube,
which he explained was a detonator; then he crimped it with
his teeth. He used a spike to work a hole in the third stick of

dynamite to receive the cap and fuse. He sure as hell told the truth when he said he was very good with dynamite.

We watched him shove loose clay in around the sticks, then tamp it firm with the bar. With his jack-knife he split the free end of the fuse protruding from the ground. He took a match from his pocket.

"Hold on a minute!" Musgrave said. "Where do we—what do we—how long do we . . ."

"Once it's going there should be three minutes. Plenty of time to take cover."

"What cover!" I said.

"Round the corner of the house, I suggest. You may go there now if you wish. I shall come when the fuse is ignited. They're rather difficult to start, you know—it might take several matches."

We all stayed. The fuse took only three matches. Then we ran and we threw ourselves round the corner of the Musgrave house and looked back. Peter had not run with us; he was still coming. He did it by strolling—with his hands in those sissy-looking English pants of his.

The way it told you how in *A Thousand Things a Boy Can Do*, I had begun to count to myself so that I would have a rough notion of when the three minutes would be up. I had reached fifty-and-nine when we heard the Musgrave screen door slap the afternoon stillness.

Lobbidy said, "Judas priest!"

Angus said, "He's headed for the backhouse!"

"He's got his knapsack and his Boy Scout hat and his cane on," I said. "Maybe he's just going out to get lost!"

Musgrave started round the corner of the house, but Lobbidy grabbed him back. "Let him keep going, Musgrave! Let him keep going so's he'll get into the clear!"

"He's my grampa!"

"I shall get him!"

"There ain't even one minute left!" Lobbidy said. That stopped Peter.

I had no way of telling if Lobbidy was right, for I had stopped counting as soon as the Musgrave screen door had slapped.

"He's stopped!" Angus yelled.

He had—right between the clothes-line poles and the

woodpile, on our side of the project, which meant he was no more than twelve feet from the sputtering fuse. I don't think he stopped because of our digging, but to gather spit. He shook his head and spit.

Peter launched himself round the corner of the house, and belly to the ground he ran up behind Austin's grampa. *Behind* that old man. Musgrave's grampa heard the running footsteps coming from *behind* him. They *had* finally come to get him!

He did not even look back to see who it was. After all these years I suppose he still had a pretty clear idea of who it would be. With Peter close behind him, he set a new octogenarian thirty-yard-dash record, and not the one for level ground, either: both of them hurdled the pile of sods, into and then across, then up and out of our excavation, then on to the privy. The old man jumped to safety inside and pulled the door shut. Without missing a stride, Peter pounded past and out to the prairie beyond. Out there he was still running with his head back, chin out, arms pumping, knees high, when the three sticks of sixty-percent dynamite let go.

The first effect was not sound at all. Initially the Musgrave yard was taken by one giant and subterranean hiccup; an earth fountain spouted; the four cords of wood took flight; the two clothes-line posts javelined into the air, their wires still stretched between them in an incredible aerial cat's-cradle. And the privy. And Musgrave's grampa. They leapt. Straight up. I think the bottom of the backhouse must have lifted six feet from ground level.

The privy was the first thing to return to earth, and when it fell its descent obeyed Newton's Law of Falling Backhouses, which says: "A falling privy shall always come to rest upon the door side." The corollary: "A loved one trapped within cannot be taken out on the vertical, only through the hole and upon the horizontal."

After the lambasting explosion we looked at each other wildly; we swallowed to unbung our ears, heard the lovely Japanese chiming of glass shards dropping from every Musgrave house window, the thud of wood chunks returning to earth. I saw Musgrave lick with the tip of his tongue at a twin blood yarn unravelling from his nostrils. No one said anything; we simply moved as a confused body in the direction of the backhouse. And Musgrave's grampa.

We had to go out and around the great, shallow saucer the dynamite had blown in Musgraves' back yard, and I remember thinking, "They're never going to ever fill that in." How could they? To get the thousands of cubic feet of dirt to fill that crater, they would have to dig another hole to get an equal quantity of dirt to fill in the new hole. And another— and another—

It was not all that deep, possibly four feet at the centre, but it was wide; if we had completed the project it would have taken all the lumber from a grain elevator to roof it in. I'm certain it would have been the biggest cave dug in southern Saskatchewan that summer.

It took all of us to upright the privy and Musgrave's grampa. When we opened the door to let the poor old man out, he was not grateful. He swung at us with his cane a couple of times before he would let Musgrave and Lobbidy help him to the house and into his room off the kitchen. Seated there on a Winnipeg couch, he stared straight ahead as Musgrave removed his Boy Scout hat, slipped off his knapsack, then with an arm around the old man's shoulders eased him down on the pillow. He motioned us out of the room.

IV

We were all whipped, of course; it was difficult to keep a thing like that quiet. As well, each of us was quarantined in his own yard. Until then the maximum punishment had been one week. Peter and the Liar and Lobbidy Lon and Angus and I received two-week sentences. Austin got three. Since it was summer holidays the punishment was much more severe than during a school term, when classes would have been a daily reprieve from nine to four. Actually I served a week, Peter the same time. Lobbidy did only four days, unless they trapped him in his grandmother's yard in Havre down in Montana, where he always spent his vacations. Musgrave had to finish the whole sentence, of course.

I was paroled, not so much for good behavior as for careful acting. I cultivated unusual restraint, deliberate and consistent quietness. It was easy never to laugh or smile. In the bathroom mirror or the one in my bedroom I practised expressions of sorrow and of sadness and—later on—pain. I wasn't optimistic about the effect on my father, who was away most of the day and not nearly so susceptible as my mother, who was always concerned about my appetite, my temperature, my regularity, my dressing warmly, taking my cod-liver oil. There were advantages to being small for my age and what was known as a "peaked child"; I must have been very young when I found out that my mother was deer-alert to coughs and sniffles. Through practice I had learned to run up a temperature at will, to make myself pale, nauseated, constipated, or loose with diarrhea, to avoid some unpleasant reckoning—more often than not an arithmetic test.

It just happened that I was well prepared for quarantine;

the root cellar under the basement stairs was well stocked with candles, last year's *Chums*, which Peter had lent me, and all of Gaboriau's novels from my father's library. The five-pound *Chums* alone, with its cigarette-paper-thin pages, was enough reading to do me for a month's quarantine. I was not alone in there; with me were English public-school boys who wore gowns or blazers and silk top hats, were at constant war with the townies, all cheats and liars and bullies working as butcher- or delivery-boys. They didn't stand a chance against the India-rubber boy and the magician and the ventriloquist.

It was quite lovely in there with the faint ferment of earth and mildew and reluctant vegetable ghosts. Candle after candle flickered while I read of dons and fags and forms, of secret night feasts after lights out: sweets and meat pies and treacle tarts and ginger beer. For some strange reason these Dionysian dormitory feasts punishable by caning were illicit. If not immoral. When English boys were not feasting or going on paper chases or being caned, they confounded German spies, who heliographed zeppelins and submarines with pocket mirrors winking from chalk cliffs. English boys got lost on misty moors, sucked into quicksand; they had it so much luckier than we did. Peter Deane-Cooper must have just hated it when his parents brought him to Canada.

There was nothing frightening at all left on our great grass sea, just coyotes and badgers and weasels, grasshoppers and gophers and harmless garter-snakes, frogs and blood-suckers, darning needles and meadowlárks. In our prairie world only other boys were dangerous. Or Airedales and Vonneguts' Holstein bull. Or adults.

Within a week, before I got to the Gaboriau novels, I had achieved a mushroom pallor, mastered a low-grade but persistent cough, and felt that a blue tint was beginning to show under my eyes. A few more days in the root cellar would have grown really great shadows, but my mother caved in. Peter was loosed the same Friday afternoon. I never remembered to ask him if his father had caned him for swiping the three sticks of dynamite.

The second cave was Peter's idea. He suggested it the very day of our release. He said that because Lobbidy and Musgrave and the Liar were out of circulation we had a marvellous opportunity to dig a cave of our own in total secret. Just us. If we were extremely careful we could get it finished without another soul's knowing we had it. I was quite flattered that Peter had picked me to be in on the new and secret cave—just me—nobody else. I was more than flattered; I was moved. Then, as I thought it over, I was surprised; I wondered if he would have chosen me if Lobbidy hadn't been sent down to be with his Montana grandmother for the rest of the summer. I didn't bother to ask him.

We knew we were going to have to be extremely careful and clever if we were to keep our cave secret from everybody else. And lucky. Location was critical; it must be well away from the usual trails taken by boys out on the prairie, yet it must be near the Mental hole or there was no sense in digging one at all. It couldn't be in a crop field where some farmer in late summer might crash through the cave roof with a binder, or in fall with a threshing machine. Vonneguts' pasture was no good, either, because a horse or a cow from their dairy herd might plunge through and have to be shot because of a broken leg. We decided finally on Muhlbiers' place on the west side of the river and downstream towards the Mental. They ran only sheep. The next problem—getting and carrying out roof boards without being seen by anyone— turned out to be no problem at all, because near the site we had finally picked for our cave was an abandoned homesteader's shack, a small one which might have once been a harvest cook-car or a bunkhouse on wheels, but was now mounted on skids like a stoneboat. You could tell it hadn't been used for years, so there wasn't anything wrong with ripping off all the boards we needed for our cave roof.

We picked Saturday afternoon to start the cave because the picture-show matinee was William S. Hart in *The Cold Deck*, so that except for us there couldn't possibly be a boy out at the Mental hole or the CPR. Just as much as anybody else, I hated to miss William S. Hart, but Peter said it wasn't a cowboy show really, because William S. Hart was only a riverboat gambler. All the same—he was still William S. Hart. If it had been Fatty Arbuckle or Buster Keaton or Lon Chaney I wouldn't have minded quite so much.

Peter said we had better start out from different parts of the edge of town, that I must go north to the end of our block, while he went west across town from his house. That way, if someone did see us, it would be just Peter carrying

the pick or me carrying our spade and roundnose shovel. I
said that would only double the chances of somebody's seeing
one of us, which was just as bad as seeing both of us. Peter
said all right then, he'd head for the back of our house and
then we'd go together from there. Nobody did see us, except
maybe Mrs. Judge Hannah in their McLaughlin, coming in
from the golf course, I guess, and she didn't even look at us.
Peter said we should take a big loop out by the Mental to
throw people off the scent.

We were quite well informed about the South Saskatchewan
Mental Hospital, for almost every family had a father or a
mother or an aunt or an uncle or a cousin or a brother or a
sister who worked out there. This slightly removed community on the north-west edge of town had its own power plant,
dairy and beef herd, gardens, greenhouses, tennis courts,
bakery, laundry, pharmacy, and moving-picture theatre. Most
crafts and trades were represented: plumbers, carpenters,
electricians, agriculturalists. Shops turned out leather goods,
baskets, furniture, pillows, and quilts. They had their own
baseball team, hockey team, and orchestra. When it came to
bridge parties and teas I suppose one out of every four such
events my mother attended was out at the Mental, in the two
blocks of staff houses built there for the doctors, nurses,
administrative heads, technicians, and attendants. There were
also patients.

We knew most of the patients who were allowed out, for
they seemed to be drawn toward the river to watch us
swimming at the Mental hole in the summer or skating there
in the winter. Several of them we knew by name: Horny
Harold, Buffalo Billy, Blind Jesus, Isaac the bird. Even
though we thought of insanity as a dreadful magic trick that
had been played on some, we said that such people *went* or
had *gone* crazy. Somehow love was involved; a mother went
crazy because her son had taken on bad ways; the unkindness
or cruelty or infidelity of a husband could put his wife into
the Mental. Eddie Crozier of Crozier's Men's Wear had done
this to Mrs. Crozier, who used to belong to my mother's
bridge club. When women patients were allowed out for a
walk with one or two attendants herding them rather like
geese, Mrs. Crozier would often be there wearing her black
karakul fur coat in winter with a toque pulled down over her
ears, or in summer a jumbo sweater-coat with her fists

punched low into the pockets and brought forward like wings covering her crotch. Musgrave once told me that Eddie Crozier lusted after strange flesh, and that had driven Mrs. Crozier to slicing her throat open with Eddie's straight razor. Before she could bleed to death they found her on the bathroom floor and sewed her throat shut and put her into the Mental.

Whenever we went into King's pool hall with pop bottles to get a cent apiece for them, Eddie Crozier would generally be there, bent low over the green felt or coming out of the door to the rummy room at the back. Besides owning Crozier's Men's Wear next to my dad's shop, he was manager of the Trojans Senior Hockey Team. Mr. Nightingale seemed to go in the pool hall quite a lot, too. If it wasn't the place for kids, it seemed hardly the place for undertakers, either.

Because Peter and I went out by the Mental we were seen; however, it was only by a gaggle of male patients with two attendants. We saw them first and headed off towards a high caragana hedge, but Horny Harold yelled and pointed us out, and Buffalo Billy started to gallop towards us. An attendant ordered him right back into the flock again.

When it was all clear we left the caragana and cut off towards the river, but even before we could smell the river's marsh breath we ran into a hatch of blue darning needles. We marvelled at the levitation magic they worked with their tandem gauze wings, often just as though they had been pinned against thin air. Many were locked in intercourse. Did they like flying so much they did it while copulating, or copulating so much they did it while flying? The way Peter put it: "They flying fucking? Or are they fucking flying?" I said only Musgrave would know.

We waded the river below the Mental powerhouse dam, then moved like young prairie dolphins over and under and over barbed-wire fences to our projected cave site.

At first the cave went well; we got all the sods up and carefully stacked, and the topsoil was such easy digging we decided to make our cave half as big again as we had started out with. For almost two feet we didn't even have to use the pick. Then we hit the hardpan. It was rock hard. We took turns on the pick. At first I hoped Peter wouldn't suggest dynamite again, then I rather wished he would. He didn't. I wanted to suggest we quit an hour earlier than we did, for I was starving and it was going to be difficult explaining why I hadn't come home a *little* after dark instead of *away* after dark.

"All right," Peter said, "let's knock it off. Tomorrow at daybreak."

"Tomorrow's Sunday."

"That is correct. Daybreak tomorrow."

"Uh-uh."

"Why not?"

"I got to go to Sunday school."

"Oh." I guess he hadn't thought of that, because the Anglicans always had their Sunday school in the afternoon. "I shall come out at daybreak," Peter said. "You come out just as soon as you can."

"Yeah—after Sunday school."

"*Before* Sunday school."

"I got to go to Sunday school.

"Then just start out for it but miss it. You *have* missed Sunday school before—haven't you?"

"Mmm-hmh."

"Well then."

For over one and a half years I had not missed Sunday school a single time. I belonged to the Cross and Crown. A year and a half before, I had won a Bible for unflawed attendance and also a Cross and Crown badge I could wear on the lapel of my Sunday suit. This was a slippery enamel lozenge, white with a scarlet cross encircled at the top by a gold crown. It looked very valuable. The only absences excusable were those caused by truly serious disease: infantile paralysis, typhoid, terminal consumption. This year I was trying for the gold wreath that would snap around my first-year badge. For each succeeding perfect year I intended to win the narrow gold banner that would hook and hang from the gold wreath; only adult maturity would stop me from having them chaining down to my belly button.

Our cave certainly buggered that up.

Right after porridge I headed for the side door, but before I could even get it open, my mother called from the breakfast room. I yelled back, "What!"

She waited a moment; then she called me again.

I yelled back, "What!" again.

"When I call you—don't you shout back 'what' to me!"

I waited. For further clarification.

"Come here!"

I did.

"Where do you think you're going?"

"Out."

"That is not an answer."

"Sunday school."

She looked up to the breakfast room clock. "Sunday school isn't for two hours."

"Hour and a half."

"So?"

"I thought I'd go there early—this morning."

"Why?"

I almost said: so I could get first pick of the Rover Boys or Horatio Alger, Jr., in the Sunday-school library; then I realized that by missing Sunday school I wouldn't be able to bring home any books at all, and she would be sure to notice and ask me why. "I don't want to be late and spoil any chances on perfect attendance this year for the gold wreath to go around my cross-and-crown badge."

"You polished your shoes?"

I hadn't.

"Have you got a clean handkerchief?"

I hadn't.

"Have you got your collection?"

I hadn't.

In spite of her tripping me up, I still got away a good hour early.

Musgrave was nowhere in their yard when I passed their corner. I couldn't see him looking out of their living-room window either. Just his grampa. I wondered if they'd let Musgrave loose for Sunday school. Probably not. The next block over from Musgraves' I turned right again so that I was walking up the street in the wrong direction to Knox Presbyterian, and it was as though the whole church pulled on the back of my head like a magnet.

Halfway down the block I passed the Catholic church, their mass was all over. I almost wished I were Catholic so that what I was doing wouldn't be quite so bad.

According to Musgrave all Catholics broke the fourth commandment. Chronically. They competed for eternal damnation with masses, holy water, incense, rosaries, alcoholic vine and wafers, candles and crucifixes; they raced and they hurdled and pole-vaulted over venial and mortal sin with confession and penance. Musgrave was extremely well informed about them; from him you got the impression that each Sunday all over the world Catholics lined up crouched and waiting for the Pope to fire off his noon starting-pistol to begin another field-day of Catholic wickedness. Just the swimming events, fresh or salt water, were left over for the Baptist Sunday.

On the second barbed-wire fence after the Mental, I caught the seat of my Sunday pants. Just a small tear. I was more careful after that.

Peter was already out there, lifting the pick high over his head, then levering the handle back and forth to pry chunks out of the hardpan. The sweat was just running down his face when he looked up to me and said he'd been there since daybreak. I said he hadn't got down very far though, had he. He said it was bloody hard digging now and it was bloody well time for me to take over the bloody pick and bloody well find out for myself how bloody hard it was! I took off my Sunday jacket and blouse. It did seem to go much faster with both of us taking turns on the pick and the shovel. We reassured each other that we'd finish in time to get home for Sunday dinner.

We were wrong. It was much harder digging than in Musgraves' back yard, and this time there were half as many diggers for a projected cave half again as big. When my back and arm muscles cried and my shoulder sockets ached more than I could stand, I would make an excuse to lay down the pick or the shovel to take another measurement, or another leak, or another sweep with the field-glasses. They were Peter's father's from the war and so powerful you had to rest on your elbows and hold your breath. They revealed that, except for humans, the prairie was well populated that Sunday morning: a badger with his raggedy hide swinging, a weasel, two coyotes, four jack-rabbits, meadowlarks, red-winged blackbirds, goshawks and . . .

"Peter!"

"Yes?"

"Somebody—way off—towards Brokenshell!"

"Give me the glasses!"

"Maybe not coming this way . . ."

"I said—let me have them!"

I handed them over to him. They were his father's
glasses. Now I could see the far-off dot with my naked eye.

"You're right!" Peter said.

"They coming our way?"

"Can't tell."

"Who is it!"

Peter was turning the thing in the centre to adjust the
focus; since I'd been the last to use the field-glasses they
didn't fit his eyes. If he'd let me keep them I could have seen
clearly who it was by now. "Well—who is it, Peter?"

"A girl."

"Huh!"

"But I can't tell who—she must be coming this way . . ."

"Let me have them!"

He took them down and handed them to me, but when I
looked through them everything was all blurred. Once I got
them focussed to match my eyes, I saw the girl and over her
head what looked like a red butterfly.

"Irma Van Wart!"

"Get down!"

I dropped flat beside Peter. "Is she really so close you
can tell—for certain?"

"Red hair-ribbon—got to be Irma."

"We'll just stay down then—if she's still far away. If we
don't move, she may not even see us. Give me the glasses—"

"You'll just have to change them again."

"Then you keep her in sight. Whatever is she doing out
here!"

That was English for what was *any* girl doing out here.
Just because of our names Irma sat right in front of me at
Haig School. She always had her hand up. She wasn't a
finger-snapper or a loose-wristed flailer; she was a telephone-
poler. She ran her arm up to its full length, the other hand
clutching just under her armpit and shoving and holding her
arm up as though it couldn't stay up there all by itself. She
always stiffened her right leg out into the aisle for better
purchase; this must have improved her hand height by lifting
the right cheek of her fat ass at least four inches off the desk
seat. She did this whenever she thought she had the right
answer or she wanted to ask a question or she needed
permission to leave the room. Irma knew everything about

everything. She finished your own sentences for you. Wrong. And she never shut up. As well, she smelled ever so faintly, but always, of horse manure.

She had a very good reason for this: her father was the town fire-chief and the family lived over the fire-station stables in the town hall. Every noon the fire-bell would go off under the Van Warts, the two stable doors would swing open, and the two fire-wagon teams would clop out of their stalls to stop on either side of the wagon tongues directly under the harness suspended from the station ceiling. The harness would descend onto their gray dappled backs and rumps. Chief Van Wart and Charlie Spinks would each go to a team, and buckle the harness under the horses and hook up the traces. They would all stand for a minute; then, like a film reversed, drop traces, unbuckle, harnesses rise, horses back up into their stalls, doors close. The daily excitement of such firedrills, and, of course, actual fires, was quite wasted on someone like Irma.

And it was Irma I had in the field-glasses all right. Instead of the Dutch-bob haircuts most girls had, Irma had long blonde curls dropping in front of her ears and hanging all the way around the back of her neck. She always wore a large silk-ribbon bow, so the effect was that of a gargantuan scarlet butterfly that had fluttered too close to her head and got stuck in those dangling fly coils. The fire-horse teams also had red ribbon braided into their manes and their club tails.

"Straight for us!" I said.

"I know—I know!"

"What we going to do!"

"You get up," Peter said. "No—don't. You *crawl*—fast as you can away from here—over to the left. Then jump up and run to her. . . ."

"Huh!"

He punched me on the shoulder. "Do as I say!"

"I got no blouse on!"

"Put it on, then! I shall stay flat! Give me those glasses! She's still far enough away she can't see what we're doing yet—move! You must decoy her away from here!"

He was right. I got a couple of buttons done on my blouse and started crawling off to the left, but it wasn't easy to snake like that and still keep her in sight. The trick was to cover as much ground away from our cave site as possible to stop her getting near enough so she could see what Peter and I were doing.

When I couldn't put it off any longer I jumped up.

"Hey—Irma!"

She stopped.

I ran towards her—not in a direct line but angling off to the left so that I could suck her over and further away from our cave site. Killdeer mothers do it all the time to protect their young. Irma didn't suck very well.

"Just what are you doing out here, Irma?"

"What are you?"

Besides finishing sentences for other people, she had a habit of answering questions with questions.

"Fooling around."

"On Sunday!"

"Sunday for you too, isn't it?" It was even *more* Sunday for her. The Van Warts were Holy Rollers.

"I'm *supposed* to be out here."

"Huh!"

"With Jesus."

"Huh!"

"I walk with Him *every* day—especially Sunday."

"Oh." Then I remembered how the Holy Rollers started up their church camp every summer as soon as school closed. At Brokenshell Grove.

"Aren't those your Sunday clothes you've got on?"

"Yeah."

"All right," she said. She had her stockings rolled down to her ankles.

"I just thought I'd..."

"...miss Sunday school to go swimming."

"No!"

"Then why are you out here?"

"None of your business."

"Who else is with you?"

"None of your business."

"You better get back to Sunday school."

"Too late now—be all over by the time I got back." I had to say something to put her off the track.

"You aren't just fooling around out here."

"How's it going with the—your—Holy Roller camp?"

"There will be a fruitful harvest of souls saved for Jesus."

"Sure," I said, "hundred bushels to the acre." I couldn't help it; the way she was so superior all the time just put your teeth on edge. I shouldn't have said it, especially on Sunday.

Her mouth tightened up. "I know you're out here with somebody else."

"Do you know your stockings are rolled down just like brown doughnuts round your ankles?"

She just stared at me.

"Does Jesus like brown stocking doughnuts?"

"Your Sunday suit's all dirty—like your soul."

She turned away and started walking back towards Brokenshell. She was dead right about my soul.

I walked in the opposite direction from our cave and when Irma was almost out of sight I circled back to Peter. By then it was time to go home for Sunday dinner. I managed to get in the house and up to the bathroom to clean up and change out of my Sunday suit. My mother didn't find the tear in the pants till two weeks later.

When we got back out to the cave we ran into luck: a good two-foot layer of sandy soil.

As always we were much too optimistic, again and again measuring the depth of our excavation long before we had dug deep enough. We judged by sighting, and since there was no sense in scaling anything at all to my size, it was always my job to walk a hundred paces off, lie flat out on my belly, and look along the ground toward Peter seated in the centre of the hole. After the third or fourth check which showed the top of Peter's head still salient, I rolled over to get up—and saw the feet, brown and sinewy thin, with horn toenails. I yelled, and Peter, still sitting in the excavation, yelled, "What's the matter!

I yelled back, "It's just Jesus!"

He was only a couple of yards from me. If I hadn't started to get up he would have tramped right on me because I hadn't heard him coming barefoot through the grass. Blind Jesus never looked down or even out—always up. To the sun. Right now he was looking to the west, with his arms held outstretched in the crucified position but with his hands open and turned up as though they were waiting for raindrops to declare themselves upon his asking palms.

Besides going crazy, Blind Jesus had made himself blind by keeping his head tilted back and his eyes to the sun. One time out at the Mental hole Lobbidy turned him halfway around and then stepped back. Blind Jesus' head moved slowly in a tropistic arc till it found the sun again, the rest of his body following afterwards. Then Austin did it. Then the Liar. Then everybody took turns doing it, until Buffalo Billy got too upset.

In spring and summer and fall Blind Jesus wore a gown; it was just like a hospital gown, but white instead of the pale green they put the patients in. Most of the time it was quite clean and there was a gold crucifix hanging down his breast-bone. With his long hair and beard he looked just about the way Jesus should look according to the stained-glass window in Knox Presbyterian, and pictures of Him in our Sunday-school paper. His eyes weren't right, though; I don't think Jesus had blue eyes.

Peter had to stop Blind Jesus before he walked into our hole, and by then Buffalo Billy had cantered up. Buffalo Billy didn't usually let Blind Jesus range too far away from him. You would swear he really was Buffalo Bill, with his buckskin jacket fringed like his gloves, which had funnelled gauntlets with a little scarlet star embroidered on each of them. He had holsters and six guns. Toy cap-pistols. His hair hung down to his shoulders and was blond, like his mustache and goatee. The toes on his riding boots were broken and the backs and sides of their high heels worn right down so he walked on the sides of his feet. Actually he seldom walked; he trotted or he galloped most of the time, making giddy-yup as well as whinny sounds. His skin was almost as dark as Jesus': heart-wood walnut. His eyes were quite blue too. Most of us liked him and asked kindly after his horse or if he'd shot many Indians or buffalo lately. This time Peter just said, "All right, Billy, just you take Blind Jesus and both of you bugger off."

He did, and a little later when we went over to the homesteader shack to pry off boards I said to Peter maybe now people would find out we had our cave, and he said no they wouldn't, because Blind Jesus couldn't tell anybody and if Buffalo Billy did, nobody would believe him because he was crazy.

I said, "I been wondering about something. You think people with blue eyes can go crazy easier than other people can?"

"No."

"I don't know—Buffalo Billy's got blue eyes. You can tell Blind Jesus' eyes used to be blue. Musgrave's grampa, his eyes are pale blue—like buttermilk."

"Coincidence. Careful with that tarpaper. It's quite brittle and we're going to need every bit of it we can save."

"You figure Blind Jesus thinks he's Jesus, Peter?"

"I don't know."

"Did he ever claim he was Jesus? Or did somebody just nickname him Jesus?"

"No idea."

"What do you think?"

"I suspect not."

"That he doesn't know it—think it?"

"He doesn't even know he's blind."

"Oh."

I kept on thinking about him while we laid down the boards for our cave roof and covered them over with tarpaper before we could start spreading out the soil and fitting the sods back together.

"I wonder why they let him loose like that?"

"Who?"

"Blind Jesus. He could wander onto the railroad tracks— get hit by a train. Walk right off the bridge, drown, get lost, starve. . . . "

"Buffalo Billy always looks after him."

"That's no way—one crazy person looking after another crazy person."

"It's why they call it the Mental, isn't it?"

I could tell that Peter wasn't really interested, and I decided I'd ask King. He knew all about crazy people, because right after the war for a couple of years he'd been an attendant out there, before he got the pool hall. Except for the tunnel entrance and for tramping down the sods better, we had the cave nearly finished. We put the pick and the spade and shovel inside and headed for home.

V

Peter and I did not discuss whether or not we should let King in on our cave; without telling each other, we knew that both of us wanted to share it with him. Just as surely as we knew we did *not* want Austin Musgrave snooping around within a hundred miles of it. After we had fitted the last sod into place and gone to the Mental hole for a clean-up swim and found King there, we told him about our cave and we asked him to come and see it.

He gave us a ride to the homesteader shack. We climbed down from the McLaughlin.

"It's west of here," I said. "We were wondering if you could find it."

"Figure I can't?" King said.

"We hope you can't," Peter said.

"Well, let's see." King looked out over the flat and empty prairie sod—then walked straight to our cave!

"Aw shit!"

"However did you do that?" Peter said.

"Simple. You told me it was west of the shack. All I needed to know. I just looked for the biggest bush there was—the one you needed to hide your tunnel entrance. Come on, you fellows—you've done a great job of camouflage. Nobody's ever going to find your cave in a million years."

Head first we crawled down the tunnel on our bellies and our working elbows, then lighted candles to show King our sanctuary secret. The roof boards were a good foot clear of King's head.

"Roomy," King said. He lit up a Millbank. "Comfortable as any trench I ever had the pleasure of being in."

"Give us a puff," Peter said.

"Nothing doing."

"Aw, King!"

"Don't start—till you're fourteen." He exhaled. "Stunt your growth, Hughie."

"It was Peter asked—not me!"

"All right—all right." He laid his head back against the wall.

"Did you ever get frightened in the trenches?" Peter said.

"All the time," King said.

"Oh." Peter sounded rather disappointed.

"Everybody gets scared," King said. "Nothing wrong with that. Main thing is—how do you handle it."

"How?" Peter said.

"By not thinking."

"I find that difficult to . . ."

"But it's right—you got to turn off thinking—right off—and do what you got to do. If you think about it, then you'll get more and more scared and more and more paralyzed. So—blank it out—thinking. That's the way the army works."

"Is it really?" Peter said.

"Yep. Mainly what the army teaches a man—not to think. It works in war. Thinking has lost and *not* thinking has won more wars than anything else."

"Why'd you have to tell me smoking would stunt my growth!"

"All right, Hughie."

"Did it stunt yours?"

"No."

"How come?"

"Because I didn't smoke when I was a little fart."

I didn't really care any more—once I'd let him know he hadn't got away with it.

It was such an earth-cool refuge down there, away from the desert sun and wind above us, that we sat contentedly, in no hurry to move, with our knees up and our backs against the cave walls. We talked while the candles cried their hot tears of wax down the backs of our hands to harden there.

When you peeled it off it was as though the wax had grown its own fine hairs.

"King—how come people go crazy?" I had got to thinking about Blind Jesus and Buffalo Billy and the way they had discovered Peter and me digging our cave. "Horny Harold and Blind Jesus and Buffalo Billy and Mrs. Crozier—what drives people crazy?"

"Other people."

"How?"

"All kinds of ways."

"What kinds of ways?"

"Oh—ah—one way—by asking questions all the time—by asking one question and when they answer that question..."

"Awww..."

"...there's another question and then another question..."

"Why should that drive a person..."

"Just like you been doing and you're doing right now...."

"No—I didn't!"

"See, you don't even know you're doing it. 'No—I didn't'—that is the very first thing you've said the past five minutes that is not a question."

"Anything wrong with that?"

"See, another question."

"Well—is there?"

"Way you do it—all the time."

"Oh. Mind if I ask you another one?"

"Shoot."

"Have I succeeded?"

"Huh?"

"In driving *you* crazy!"

He laughed. "You mean little son of a bitch! Hughie—Hughie—Hughie—I just thought I'd bring it to your attention."

"Thanks, King."

He put his arm around my shoulder. I pushed it off.

"There is one other way," King said.

"What's that?" Peter said.

"Who gives a shit!" I said.

"People can drive other people crazy," King explained, "by getting mad at people and then sulking every time somebody tells them something they don't want to know."

"That so!"

"Yep. It is so."

"I am not sulking!"

"And another way—contradicting people."

"Aw—come on, King!"

"And another way is—people that are too serious and haven't got a sense of humour so they cannot recognize when somebody who *has* a sense of humour is just having some fun."

"You making fun out of me!"

"No—there is a difference between making fun *of* a person and just making fun. I was making fun."

"Oh."

"Partly."

"You know something, King—I know a way that people can send other people crazy—by pretending they are answering somebody's question when all the time they are just putting up a smoke-screen to keep from answering people's questions."

"I see." King drew back his lips and he clicked his teeth a few times. "All right, Hughie. There are a lot of things—being lonely is one of them. Having the shit scared out of you on a regular basis might be another. Or realizing nobody thinks you're worth a shit. Or worse, knowing it yourself. There is one main one, though."

"What's the main one, then?" Peter said.

"Being a human."

"How does that work?" I asked him.

"It just does—being a human."

"Don't animals go crazy," Peter said. "Ever?"

"You get mad dogs," I said, "but that's out of a germ." We'd taken that up in Hygiene when they told all about Pasteur.

"Let's put it this way. Humans—without the benefit of germs or disease—can go crazy. Just out of being humans."

"Not all humans, King," I said. "There's lots don't go crazy. How come they don't?"

"Lucky," King said. "Just goddam lucky!"

We pinched out our candles and crawled above.

"I'd get some gunnysack," King advised. "Make a frame out of lath the size of that entrance hole. Cover it with your burlap—no, even better—you get some chicken wire and weave dead grass or straw through the holes. Use that—works great on goose pits, and anything that can fool a Canada honker can sure fool a human."

"I remember seeing chicken wire recently," Peter said after King had let us out in front of the pool hall. "It was a couple of weeks ago behind Thomas's. I rather think it might still be there against the fence."

It wasn't, though you could see where Mr. Thomas had done over the chicken coop for his white Wyandots. Before we headed out to the town garbage dump, we picked up a lot of good turkey feathers for making darts out of corks and horseshoe nails and for fletching arrows. There was lots of old chicken wire out at the dump, as well as a dead horse with maggots and a stuffed moose head. I couldn't see a single thing wrong with that moose head and I thought how nice it would look on the wall in my father's den.

But Peter had seen it first and was bending over it. "This is going up on my wall," he said, "right over the bed." As he lifted it, little gray moths flew out of its ears and nostrils, and I didn't argue with him about who saw it first, because I knew right away how delighted my mother would be if I brought home a moose head to infest her closets and drawers. Peter set it down a few steps away from the garbage pile. "Why would anyone throw out a perfectly fine moose's head?" I didn't tell him that moths were a perfectly fine reason for throwing out a moose's head.

Later, after we'd found two beer and three pop bottles he said, "All yours, Hughie—you let me have the moose's head." I suppose I should have warned him then about the moths, but I was pretty sure his mother would, and he might be able to solve the problem by stuffing moth-balls down the moose's nostril- and ear-holes.

We made a lot of other valuable finds: a car battery, several lengths of one-inch galvanized pipe, a rusted coal-oil lantern, all but the glass chimney, a wash boiler that must have at least four pounds of copper in it, and a Big Ben alarm clock. The glass was gone; its mainspring had given up and the minute hand was missing, but the alarm spring was still alive, and if you pushed the hour hand around to seven, the bell would still go off. Also, inside there would be all those lovely, spindled cogs that put me in mind of little brass daisies. I had seen the clock first.

Nearer the center of the garbage dump we found three soggy and mildewed pillows; their striped ticking was torn, but they still had most of their feathers. Dried out in the sun they would be just great for sitting on in our cave. We cut the tongues out of two pairs of boots we found; leather for slingshot pockets. Just as we were about to give up picking through the heaps, Peter saw something almost buried under a pile of mattress and cardboard: a wicker baby carriage with four perfectly good wheels. While we were pulling it free, I spotted the flashlight; it still had its thick, cambered lens glass for magnifying the sun's heat and starting fires.

We piled everything into the wash boiler and lifted it up onto the baby carriage to wheel our cargo back to Peter's house. By the time we had taken the pop bottles, the copper boiler, and the car battery to Mr. Pollock's junk yard, it was too late to go out to the cave. Fifty-seven cents. It was astonishing what adults threw away!

We still had time to buy a bottle of pop at the pool hall. When we got there, Eddie Crozier was talking to King behind the counter.

"He had handcuffs and leg irons on," Eddie said.

"Not likely," King said. "Strait-jacket maybe."

"They found the basement cell empty early this morning."

"I know."

"Padded one," Eddie said. "His fifth escape."

"Fourth," King said. "What you kids want?"

"Pop," I said. "Lemon."

Peter said, "Orange."

I said, "Who escaped?" I didn't have to ask out of where, because there was only one place in our town where they had padded cells in the basement. I really didn't have to ask who it was either. It had to be Bill the Sheepherder.

"Mounties didn't get in touch with you, eh?" Eddie said.

"They did."

"You going to help them?"

"I told them I couldn't spare the time if Bill was going to make a hobby out of escaping."

"How the hell did he do it this time? Fourteen-foot ceiling—high window with heavy strap mesh?" Having his wife in the Mental seemed to keep Eddie Crozier pretty well informed.

"He lifted the metal pail out of his sanitary toilet," King said. "He set it on top of the toilet and climbed up on top.

Used a tablespoon to dig out at the base of the iron straps."

"Still take a lot of luck," Eddie said. "Maybe he had outside help."

"Sure he did," King said, "the contractor."

"Huh!"

"Shorted the Provincial Government on their concrete mix when they built the Mental."

"He can be dangerous," Eddie said.

"GPI's are always dangerous. If you hit them on a wrong day they can hurt you bad."

"What's a GPI?" I said.

"One way of being crazy. You kids drink up your pop. Stay out of pool halls."

On the way home I said I'd drop by Peter's house early in the morning so we could fix up the cave opening with the chicken wire and lath. I didn't know then that the next afternoon was my mother's turn to have the IODE, which meant my whole morning was going to be shot, beating the carpets out on the clothes-line, then mopping and dusting and waxing the living room, the music room, the dining room, the den, and the breakfast room so the whole house smelled like a beehive. It did not bother my mother at all that this was girls' work. She said she was sorry she hadn't provided me with a sister and that she and Hertha were busy in the kitchen, making sandwiches and brownies and ladyfingers and mocha cakes. I was also to do the crystal prisms on the dining-room chandelier, and why did it always have to be a battle to get me to do anything around the house. I said maybe it was because it was girls' work and she said I was repeating myself.

I left the carpets to the last so that I could get the housework over before Peter dropped by and caught me at it. Also, there was something nice about swatting the carpets with the wire beater as hard as I could *after* all that dusting and mopping and waxing. When I had taken the carpets back inside and laid them out, my mother checked and said I had done a good job; even though it wasn't Saturday when she would give me a dime for the Hi-Art matinee, she gave me a quarter. She knew how to make a person feel ashamed of himself. I headed for Peter's house.

Going out to our cave, Peter and I circled wide around the Mental and CPR swimming-holes in case anybody out there might wonder why we were carrying three pillows and lath and a roll of chicken wire out onto the prairie. We dropped everything by the rosebush.

"Hold up!"

Peter, who had started into the tunnel, pulled back.

"What's the matter?" I said.

He pointed down and I squatted beside him. He grabbed his nose between his fingers the way you do when you smell something bad. I caught it right away then; besides the smell of earth and cured grass and sage, there was something else. Peter took me by the arm as he stood up, then pulled me away from the tunnel entrance. "There's somebody down there," he whispered.

"Oh, no!"

"What's that smell, then?"

"I don't know."

"But you did smell it?"

"Yeah."

"Well then!"

"I don't know. I've smelled something like it—stronger—but I don't know ... "

"I heard before I smelled!"

"What!"

"Rather like bumping—against the roof boards, perhaps! Somebody's in our cave, Hughie!"

I knew he was right; I didn't want to know it, but I knew it. We hadn't even used our secret cave, and now somebody had discovered it and spoiled it! "Maybe it's not anybody," I said. "Maybe it's just some animal crawled down there."

"Fox!" I could tell Peter wanted to believe that too. "Badger—prairie wolf!" peter always called coyotes prairie wolves. He jumped over to the tunnel opening. "Get out of there! That's our cave!" which was a hell of a way to talk to a prairie wolf.

He came back to me. "It's no animal! Eczema ointment!"

"Huh!"

"That smell! The Liar!"

The Liar had eczema all right and he did smear it with ointment, and the smell that breathed faintly from our cave mouth did remind me of the Liar's. "He's still under quarantine."

"Unless they freed him—this morning!"

"They didn't."

"Russell!" He was back at the cave entrance. "We know it's you, Russell!"

"No, it isn't, Peter."

"Get out of there! You are trespassing on our cave!"

"I saw him in their back yard this morning."

"Rotten luck! Maybe it's King."

"Where's his car?" I hated it when something happened and there wasn't anything you could do about it. "What we going to do, Peter?" I could tell he felt helpless too, waiting for whoever it was to answer us or come out, and knowing they were not going to do either one. "I'm not crawling down inside there!"

Peter had been reaching into his side pocket. He brought out a firecracker. It was not one of the small package ones. It was a two-for-a-nickel giant cannon firecracker about four inches long and as thick as your thumb, the kind we used when we played war. I knew then what Peter had done while I was house-cleaning: spent part of his garbage-dump money in Chan Kai's.

"You can't throw that down there!"

"Certainly can. Just into the tunnel. It won't injure him—seriously."

"I wouldn't."

"It's our cave, isn't it? Doesn't look as though he's going to be coaxed out—does it?" Peter bent over the cave mouth again. "I just happen to have a stick of dynamite here! My father's—from the mine! Seventy percent! We don't want to have to blow you out, you know!" He straightened up. "Have you a match?"

"No." I was glad I didn't have one.

"Give me your magnifying glass, then."

I did have that with me. Unfortunately. I handed it down to him where he kneeled and gathered up some dry grass. "Could just as easy be some big kid, you know, Peter! Fat Isbister!"

Smoke was beginning to thread up from the dry grass as Peter focussed the glass; he bent over and began to blow on it.

"Peter—don't!" I knew there was some reason he should not throw that cannon firecracker inside of there, but I didn't know exactly what it was. I knew there was a good reason as well as I had ever known anything in my life!

A flame had been born. Peter fed it some more dry grass. The flame grew. Peter dipped the tip of the firecracker fuse into it.

"Peter!"

He threw the sputtering firecracker as far as he could down the tunnel, and just about then I realized why he shouldn't have done it.

"Bill the Sheepherder!"

Peter looked up to me and he knew I was right! I think, in the next few seconds, even though the odds were against us, we both prayed the cannon firecracker would turn out to be a dud. It didn't. The explosion was nothing like the one that blew up Austin's grampa in their back yard. In the backhouse. It was about equal to a ten-gauge goose-gun shell, strong enough to blow dirt and pebbles out of the tunnel mouth.

Peter and I decided to leave.

We ran all the way into town and to the pool hall. Except for King, on his stool behind the counter, it was empty. King was carving on a duck decoy. We told him.

"It's him—Bill the Sheepherder!"

"We're certain!" Peter said.

"Did he come out?"

"No," we said.

"Did you see him?"

"No," Peter said. "We ran after the firecracker went off."

King set the block down on the counter and folded up his jack-knife. The screen door slapped.

"Leon," King said. "Look after the tables for a while, will you."

"We found Bill the..."

"About an hour," King said. He had grabbed my arm. Tight.

"Out at our..."

King squeezed my arm and I realized he was telling me to shut up about Bill the Sheepherder.

He took Peter and me out the back way.

"Get in."

He started up the McLaughlin.

I thought he'd drive straight to the RCMP barracks or out to the Mental, but he turned up Government Road and drove past the Fairgrounds.

"Aren't we going to tell the Mounties, King?" I said.

"Let's see if it's him first," King said. "Or if he's still down in there. How long since you fellows left him?"

"Half an hour," Peter said.

"More like an hour," I said.

"But you didn't see him and he didn't see you."

"Well, he heard us," I said, "and he heard Peter's firecracker."

"If it is Bill the Sheepherder," Peter said, "wouldn't he get out just as soon as we'd left and the coast was clear?"

"Maybe not." King turned the car off Government Road. "One of you open the gate."

Peter was nearest the door. When Peter had closed the gate and got back in, King said, "He heard you up above, but he doesn't know whether you know he's the one down there...."

"That cannon firecracker that Peter..."

"Lots worse than that at Vimy and Passchendaele and the Somme—poor bastard won't be thinking too clearly anyway, and that firecracker would just reinforce his gut feeling that he's safer underground. If it's him—he'll be curled up down there. Till dark anyway."

King stopped the car by the homesteader shack. We followed him over to the rosebush. He bent down.

"Hey down there—anybody home!"

There wasn't a sound from below ground.

"Bill! You down in there, Bill? This is King!" He waited again. "Time for the showers, Bill, and a nice new clean camisole and an extra cup of cocoa!" King squatted down. "Bill!" he yelled. "Come on out now!"

I said, "What's a camisole?"

King stood up. "He's down there."

"If it's him," Peter said.

"What's a camisole?" I said.

"It's him all right."

"How can you tell?" I said.

"Smelled him."

"We did too!" Peter said.

"Then now you know why they call him the Sheepherder," King said.

"King?"

He didn't answer me, just stared down at the tunnel

entrance. He took out a cigarette package, lit one, threw the match away.

"What are we going to do?" Peter said.

"I'm not sure."

"Shouldn't we go tell the Mounties?" I said.

"What do you suppose they'll do?"

"Get him out—take him back to the Mental."

"How?" He had me there. "Drown him out? Like a gopher?"

"Take a lot of wash-tubs of water," I said.

"He is not a gopher, Hughie."

"Dig him out," Peter said.

"Well—nice neither one of you suggested they trap him. I just don't like the idea of getting Mounties and attendants and ripping him out of there." He squatted down by the tunnel entrance. "Bill! King up here! Just me and a couple of kids so it's safe for you to come out! I was just kidding about the camisole!"

"What's a camisole?"

"Strait-jacket. You all right? Can you use a smoke? How long since you ate? Answer me—goddam you!"

"I still think we ought to get the . . ."

"Shut up! Bill, if you been down there all day you must be thirsty! Come on upstairs and let's see what shape you're in! How about a nice shot of whiskey to pick you up?" He looked up to us. "We just got to convince him we're on his side."

"He's a crazy escaped patient. . . ."

"That's right, Hughie, so it isn't going to be easy to get him to trust us." He stood up. "But we will."

"How?" Peter said.

"Take a while, but we will. I want you and Peter to stay here. Keep an eye on the cave. . . ."

"Where are you going?" I said.

"Town."

"What for?"

"Canteen of water—some grub—maybe blankets."

"He's dangerous!" I said.

"He can be if he's having one of his fits."

"Was he having one when he had the whole Manyberries district held at gun . . ."

"Stay well back—just let him know you're up here and

that's all. If he starts to come out—you fellows get out of the
way. Fast!"

"Oh, we will, sir."

I guess Peter couldn't help it if he was English. English
kids were a lot different from North American kids. They
always got shall-will-will right every time and talked so
politely and called adults "sir" every time they turned around
and looked so innocent. At least you knew where you stood
with a North American kid—some of the time. No wonder
they sent them away from home to public schools to be
caned, as soon as they could after they were weaned.

After King had left, Peter said, "Isn't it just ripping!"

I said, "No!"

He had taken something out of his pocket.

"What you got there!"

He held it up.

"Put that goddam firecracker back!"

'If he starts to come out, this should drive him back
under again."

"Goddamit, Peter, this isn't the Hi-Art and Mr. Golley
playing the piano and drums!"

"It's lots better than that!"

"Yeah!" I was thinking of those Manyberries farmers
crouched in the ditch and the thirty-thirty and the Springfield
and the twenty-two and the ten-gauge on the cot. "Perfectly
fucking ripping! Tell the Manyberries farmers..."

"He's not armed."

"Put it back in your pocket, Peter!"

He put it back in his pocket.

"Where you going now!"

"To do what we came out here for in the first place." He
was bent over the chicken-wire roll; he picked up a lath and
threw it to me like a spear. "Measure the opening with this.
Might as well do something useful till King returns."

"Just a minute! He told us to keep an eye on the cave
opening and let Bill know we were up here—and that's all!"

"Are you frightened?"

"No!" I walked over to him. "I am scared shitless!" I
stared at him. "Aren't you?"

He did not answer right away and then he said, "A bit."

"A bit! A bit! You should be scared shit—"

"Same thing," Peter said.

"It is stupid to do anything to stir him up! It is also stupid for us to be standing here so somebody can see us and come over to find out what we're doing here."

"Perhaps it is."

"No perhaps! Let's go over to the homestead shack. We can keep a lookout from there."

We did that till King got back.

"He make a move?" King said after he climbed out of the McLaughlin.

"No."

"Never took our eyes off him, sir," Peter said.

"Good." King was getting stuff out of the back of the car.

Over at the rosebush he dropped a gray wool army blanket and a round khaki canteen and a gunnysack. He squatted down and began to pull stuff out of the sack. "We'll just shove it down in the tunnel and leave it there for him. There's water—couple pounds of wieners—cheese—loaf of bread—can of Old Stag chewing-tobacco plugs." He looked up to us. "I remembered—Bill doesn't smoke. Chews. Filthy habit."

He held up a dark bottle and looked through it. He pulled the cork and tilted it, then looked through it again. "Couple of good ones left for him." He shoved the bottle down into the tunnel opening. He stood up. "Now—wait and see." He turned and began walking towards the car.

"See what?" I said.

"What he decides."

"About what?"

"Stay or go. We'll come out tomorrow."

"What shall we do then?" Peter said.

"We'll see tomorrow."

"See what?" I said.

"Whether he comes out for us—trusts us. What shape he's in."

"Then we'll take him back to the Mental?" I said.

"Mmm-hmh." King started up the car. "If he's still in your cave."

He was. When we went out there the next morning the blanket and supplies were gone. Bill was still down below. We knew that because he grunted back when King called down to him, but he still would not come out or even show himself.

"Going to take a little more time," King said.

"I think we should go straight to the Mounties," I said. "Or the Mental."

"Isn't that simple."

"Huh! He's a crazy escaped patient!"

"That's right."

"Supposed to be in the Mental, isn't he!"

"I did not say he wasn't supposed to be, Hughie."

"They got to take care of him! If he was somebody out of an ordinary hospital you'd want to get him back there as quick as possible. . . ."

". . . and as gentle," King said. "I got no argument with you. Another day or so—we'll take him back—when it's time."

I still didn't feel right about it. Going to sleep that night I prayed that when we went out in the morning Bill the Sheepherder would be gone from our cave. I strongly suspect that Peter was praying the opposite. He won.

"We got to make out a check-list," King said. "Salt—sugar—tea—coffee—kettle—frying-pan—matches—like of that."

"Doesn't sound like we're getting him back to the Mental so the doctors and nurses can help him get better!"

"Nobody gets better in the Mental, Hughie."

"That's what it's for!"

"Supposed to be. Strait-jacket restraint and needles and hosing down and slopping around in his own shit is supposed to be very beneficial therapy."

"What's the plan, then, sir?" Peter said.

"Well, look at it this way—he went to a lot of trouble to get out. I don't see any harm in him staying down in there for a while. Having a sort of a holiday—from Ward Four."

"We'd be breaking some sort of a law. . . ."

"He's no criminal," Peter said.

"He's dangerous!"

"Don't worry, Hughie. I can—I handled him in the Mental. He needs a needle, I can give it to him just as well here as they can in the Mental. I tell you what—you fellows think it over. Make up your own mind about it." He turned toward the McLaughlin. "Let's go back to town."

In the car King said, "It's your cave. It's your decision. Whether or not you want to let him stay for a while in your cave—I don't want you ever to say I pushed you into it!" King sure was different from Mr. Mackey, or my mother, or any other adult I ever knew.

"I'm warning you it's risky. I've told you he can be dangerous. You've got to follow my orders to the letter."

"Oh, we will, sir."

"Hold on. I want you to think it over very carefully—not just overnight—couple of days. I have to go south, and when I get back will be plenty of time to make up your mind about Bill. Talk it over between you. I want you to talk it over well."

He had stopped by the depot and now he sat with hands loose at the wrists and hanging down from the top of the steering wheel. "I got a call to make on Pollock," he said. "You fellows get out here. See you when I finish my business down south of here."

"What business, sir?"

"Business in Montana that's none of your business. Two days to make up your mind and let me know. It'll also give Bill time."

"To get away," I said.

"Maybe. Maybe not. Let him decide that. Don't you two go near him or that cave. Those blankets and that grub have persuaded him to be our guest so far. If he changes his mind about staying, then that sort of decides the matter for us, doesn't it? If he stays—then it's your decision."

"I don't want it to be my decision!" I said. But he didn't seem to hear me, because the car was already moving off.

"I don't want it to be our decision!" I said to Peter.

"I do," Peter said. "Ask your mother if you can come over to our place for dinner. . . ."

"Now?"

"Tonight."

"You mean supper."

"Dinner's at night."

"This isn't England and supper sure as hell isn't at noon."

"That's correct. See if she'll let you stay overnight too and we can discuss it further then. Just as King suggested. Why do you think he visits Pollock's so often?"

"Empty pop bottles."

"Not empty," Peter said, "and not—as you call them —'pop'. Yankee business, that's what he's on!"

"He said down south—Montana—so I guess it pretty nearly has to be."

"Al Capone!" Peter said.

"Who's he?"

"Never heard of him? The famous Yankee gangster? He's the leader over all the other gangsters, matter of fact, and carries his machine-gun in a violin case. In Chicago."

"King isn't driving to Chicago and back in any two days," I said. "Just Montana."

"As I said—quite possibly Chicago, Montana."

"Chicago is not in Montana."

"Isn't it? Oh." Peter sounded quite disappointed that Chicago wasn't in Montana. "Perhaps Mr. Capone's arranged to meet King in Montana then."

"Horse shit!"

"Possibly. Possibly not. He does see a lot of Pollock though, doesn't he?"

In his cemetery-sized junk yard beside the CPR tracks, opposite the depot and slightly east of it, we visited Mr. Pollock often, to sell him junk and gopher tails. He paid cash for coyote, badger, skunk, weasel, jack-rabbit skins. He had stacks of green cow- and horse-hides and sheep fleeces in the sheds, as well as washing-machines and iceboxes and gramophones, tables and chairs and car batteries and bottles and copper and lead. Outside the sheds stood anywhere from six to a dozen old Model-T's and any number of second-hand metal beds rusting unprotected from the weather. They must have been there just as junk; nobody would ever want to sleep on them again.

In his office part Mr. Pollock weighed your copper or lead on a large scale by the door, with an arm along which he would slide a notched weight to the proper reading, while you waited anxiously, hoping and hoping the arm would stay up from horizontal. Mr. Pollock often slept in a nest under the counter, even though he had a little house on the south side by the river. If you took gopher tails in to him before school in the morning, he might be just coming up from under, and sometimes you'd find him doing the same thing in mid-afternoon, as though he'd been having a nap.

Until my father explained to me, I had not known the full extent of Mr. Pollock's operations.

"Those prohibition years Orrin Nightingale seemed to be

receiving quite a few shipments of caskets, oh, as many as six—a dozen caskets a month. Pretty high death rate for our community during the spring, summer, fall months of the year. The caskets had been shipped from Winnipeg—sometimes as far away as Montreal. They seemed to arrive in a freight car that always got shunted over to the south track there in front of Pollock's yards *before* they would be unloaded to be sent to Nightingale's Funeral Home, and they stayed there at least overnight—more like two or three days—before they got shunted back again. Also—Mr. Nightingale seemed to do just as much business in caskets going the other way—to Winnipeg and Montreal. All those empty rye, Scotch, gin, rum, beer bottles Pollock had stacked in his sheds there must have been very confusing for Inspector Kydd. Seemed strange to me, though, that two different freight agents didn't wonder about Orrin's roaring business in caskets he shipped east that were very similar to the caskets that had just been shipped out west to him the week before.

"They were all in on it together, King, Pollock, Nightingale. I did a little arithmetic one time—your average large casket would hold about one hundred quarts—in crates—twelve bottles to the crate. To be carried over the border they had to be taken from the crate and slipped into little jute bags; that way a seven-passenger McLaughlin with the back seats out would handle a hundred and eighty, maybe two hundred quarts, which cost two dollars a bottle at the distillers but in Montana went for twelve dollars a bottle. Roughly twenty-four hundred dollars for an investment of four hundred dollars—not counting freight charges both ways on the caskets, and whatever the agent was paid each time for his shunting errors. And what they drank themselves."

Before I had supper at Peter's place, my mother said I could stay over with him, and be sure not to eat with my mouth open, and make certain I laid my knife and fork evenly side by side on my plate when I was done with it, and get seconds only if I was invited to. I didn't have to worry about the last one, because Peter's father kept saying, "Another helping, lad," and piling up my plate whether I wanted it or not. It was steak-and-kidney pie, which wasn't really pie at all but a sort of pudding, which Peter said his mother took a fortnight to cook. Mr. Deane-Cooper also kept filling my milk glass till I was sloshing with it.

Peter's mother didn't say very much, but she laughed a lot at whatever I said, so I think I delighted her, and didn't make any mistakes that I knew of. Peter's father smelled like menthol and licorice. He had a funny way of talking, not just his English accent, but the way he talked made me think of a gramophone needle that kept jumping back and then playing on and then skipping back a couple of grooves. He echoed himself and said "aaah" before each echo. For instance:

"I've never smoked, you know, and I certainly hope— aaaaah—certainly hope neither of you two do, either, because it's not good for you at all—aaaaah—for you at all, which is why I never did smoke. Took up snuff instead. Underground as a young chap I found it—aaaaah—found it cleared out my sinuses wonderfully well—aaah—wonderfully well so that I've seldom if ever had cold. Head or otherwise."

I could believe that. Few cold germs could have survived all that snuff up Mr. Deane-Cooper's nose, and the ones that did would have to hang tight up in there. Because when Peter let me have a little try of it that night, I felt a cold wind blowing through my whole head, and a moment later I nearly blew my ass off, sneezing twenty-three times in a row. Peter must have known what would happen or he wouldn't have started counting right from my first sneeze. Out loud.

I wondered if snuff could stimulate hair growth, because Mr. Deane-Cooper had black tufts of it growing thick as wild oats out of each nostril, but that couldn't be right unless he was stuffing snuff into his ears as well as his nose. He had an awful lot of hair growing out of his ears, too.

That night in bed Peter and I decided we'd go along with letting Bill the Sheepherder stay in our cave. Peter had already made up his mind even before we left King. I felt a little sad about it. After all that work on it we'd never really used the cave that was to be our sanctuary—just Peter's and mine—and King's too if he wanted. I had looked forward to the candle-lit secrecy that would wind delight tighter and tighter and make it sing for me even just thinking about it—in school—in bed—just walking down the street.

So much for that.

VI

One unexcused absence from Sunday school destroyed
you for the Cross and Crown. Since I had done that when
Peter and I started our cave, missing a second or third time
should not have been as important as the first. Also, missing
Sunday school was not to be compared to playing hookey
from proper school. Yet my conscience was quite active that
summer; guilt stabbed me, especially each Sunday morning
when my mother gave me my dime for collection. By putting
them in the cigar box with the carved lid in my bottom
drawer, I was successful in not spending them. I knew that by
the time I became a practising Christian again, my contribu-
tions to both Sunday and Mission boxes would be jackpot
ones.

At first I could manage the guilt because there was also a
tight excitement that stirred in me again and again. Peter and
I and King were together in a great adventure. It frightened
and it thrilled and more than made up for the visitations of
guilt—which had not exactly been a stranger to me, in the
past.

It was more than an adventure; it was a selfless mission
for Peter and me. We had dedicated ourselves, not with the
fervor of Father Brébeuf and his brethern or Joan of Arc or
the boys who fought the war to save us from the Huns, yet
with passion all the same. It warmed me every time I thought
about Bill curled up safely underground while everybody
scoured the countryside looking for him. Because we had
hidden him, they weren't able to capture him and take him
back to the Mental and buckle him into a strait-jacket. It made
me feel quite noble, every time his name was mentioned—

and it came up often, as people discussed his impossible
escape.

When King got back from his business trip to south of
the border, Peter didn't ask him how Mr. Capone was when
he met him in Chicago, Montana. King warned us how
touchy it was going to be, hiding Bill the Sheepherder in our
cave.

"Now I want you fellows to know how it is with him,"
King said. "He can be dangerous. If you hit him on a wrong
day he could hurt you—bad. One fit he had in the Mental it
took three of us to get him down to give him a needle. So
we'll make this rule—which is not to be broken, ever: that
cave is off limits to you—unless I am with you. Understand?"

I said I did and so did Peter.

"If we're going to pull this off we got to be very careful
—we don't have to worry about him now he knows he's safe
and we're feeding him and he doesn't have to climb out of
there—except at night when it's safe. We got to worry about
somebody spotting *us*—coming or going. Law of averages—
open prairie. Though in a way we got that working for us—no
cover at all, so nobody will think anybody can be hiding
there. So—never come to the cave from the same direction
twice in a row—*after* you check out with me at the pool hall.
If I say so—all right. Then—when you get out here look for the
McLaughlin and wherever it is you head for there. From
there we work it like a patrol—one ahead to scout and give
the signal for the others to that point—then ahead again, and
catch up again and ahead again."

The cave location bothered me, the way it was between
Sadie Rossdance's three little cottages and the Fairgrounds,
right where Johnny J. Jones pitched when the circus came to
our town. For the first time in my life I was hoping it
wouldn't be a circus summer. It could be awkward to have the
tent pitched over where we had Bill hidden, or anywhere
near the cave, with hundreds of people all over the place, and
elephants to step on the cave roof. We never had advance
warning the circus was coming to town until just a couple of
weeks before it happened, when the advance agent came to
the district and pasted up the posters. I mentioned it to King
and he said the odds were pretty slim Bill would get stepped

on by an elephant, since the circus showed up only about
once in four years.

"That's one-to-three odds."

"It came last year—probably one to a hundred they hit
the same place two years in a row."

"Gipsies."

"What about them?"

"They always camp between the Fairgrounds and..."

"When did they come last time?"

"Summer before last...."

"That's right—and the time before that was 1919. Just
quit worrying about circuses and gipsies camping—unless
they happen. Worry about what we got to worry about, and
that's somebody wondering why we're out here a lot—if they
see us—or Bill. Worry about not taking any chances with
him."

Even though King kept cautioning us, it was difficult
after a while to really believe that Bill the Sheepherder could
be dangerous. He looked like a thin sheep with that puffy
look around his mouth, and the way his eyes were mottled
blue like a sheep's eyes are. He never talked, just made
sounds a lot like when you held a blade of grass between your
thumb ends and the lower joints and then blew. Sometimes
he made contemplative clicking sounds —in his throat.

Most of the time I saw just his face looking up to me
from the mouth of the tunnel. Generally his eyes did not tell
you anything; but sometimes they did, though not clearly at
all. Whatever they told, it was terrible; they would become
fixed and stark, like the eyes, I imagine, of someone looking
up to you when he is going under for the third time. Not that
they were seeking help, but they were dreadfully preoccu-
pied with survival.

I saw that look several times. Then later I saw another
one when I threw some cans of condensed milk and pork and
beans into the tunnel. I think I must have wakened him. I
heard an angry roar, then furious scrabbling. When his face
appeared in the tunnel mouth it was contorted with rage. No
mistake about what was bothering him! It was me! Just about
then I stopped feeling noble about the way we were protect-
ing him and being his lifeline.

From the beginning, he smelled; it travelled to you from
the cave and up out of the tunnel. I had never known

anything live to smell so strong, but King said Peter and I would smell just as bad if we'd been patients in the Mental. I didn't think that explained. it; there was more to it than not having a bath, even for three years. It was a thick smell that made you close off the back of your throat against the strong musk of it.

"He's awful gamey," I said.

"Sheep," King said. "Stinks just like an old ram."

I agreed to that; even though I'd never smelled an old ram up close. It was just like the Liar from the ointment he greased his eczema with. Lanolin.

"I guess we got to clean him up," King said the first Sunday we were out there. "Right now's as good a time as any for it."

He stepped over to the tunnel opening and squatted down. Bill was just inside and looking up to him. "C'mon out of there, Bill."

Bill made that hoarse bleat sound.

"C'mon now. It's all right for you to come out. And I want you to, because you're going to have a nice bath in the river."

This time the bleat meant no.

"We're going to clean you up and wash your clothes out and it'll be easier on us and nicer for you too. C'mon!"

Bill seemed to pull back into the tunnel a bit.

"I don't believe he wants to take a bath," Peter said.

"That is quite obvious! Now—you get up out of there, Bill!" King waited. "That is an order!" He just cracked it out and it was as though Bill's eyes saluted. He might even have moved forward a bit. Unintentionally. Then he sagged back. His eyes were desperate. There wasn't a chance he would obey King's command even at the barrel end of a rifle.

King made a lunge and a grab for him, but Bill sucked back and down out of sight. King dived in after him, then pulled out again. Fast.

"Jesus!" He coughed as he walked away several steps. I could see he was taking down deep breaths. He muttered something about "Vimy Ridge!" and what sounded like "Mustard gas!"

He took a final deep breath and went back to the tunnel mouth. "You are coming out of there—whether you like it or not! Your last chance! C'mon out—before I *burn* you out!"

He waited about a count of ten then looked up to Peter and me. "Willow twigs! Cow shit! Dry ones!"

Peter ran off towards the river. I began looking for cow pies, which should have been easy to find, except that Muhlbiers ran sheep mostly. Down on his knees King was clawing loose dead grass into a pile a couple of feet back from the tunnel opening. All the time he kept talking to Bill down there. "Brought this on yourself, you know. Forced us into it. We just want to clean you up—that's all —before you stink up the country from here to the correction line. Anybody coming by within a mile of here could pick up the smell and follow it right to you. We're just trying to protect you, Bill, and you're making us smoke you out—for your own good."

Talk like that sounded familiar to me: just-before-the-strap talk.

King arranged the dry willow twigs like a teepee over the dead-grass pile. He scratched a match and the grass caught, the flame licking up around the willow twigs Peter had brought.

"Started her up, Bill! You kids take off your blouses. Use them like a fan, when I tell you."

He began to add my cow pies to the fire and the smoke really lifted in clouds.

"Fan!"

Stooping with our legs apart, Peter and I fanned with our blouses to bend the sour column of smoke towards the tunnel mouth. I suppose King had built the fire upwind, but it must have shifted because my eyes were stinging. Then we heard Bill start coughing underground.

"It's getting to him!" King said.

Getting to *me!*" I made out Peter with his eyes squeezed shut, and I wished I'd thought of that. I closed mine and felt some tears slide down. We kept on flapping our blouses.

Bill started roaring and then bumping against the cave roof.

He can't take much more! When he comes—jump aside—I'll grab him!"

He didn't come out; he was bunged, just like a rock from a slingshot, fired through the smoke and aimed right for me. He hit me right in the bread-basket. With his head. I went flat on my back, and he went over the top of me.

"Don't stop him! He's headed in the right direction!" King yelled.

I rolled over and got to my knees. I couldn't get my breathing going.

"Hughie!"

"Just keep the pressure on him as long as he's going towards the river!"

Evidently King hadn't been able to grab him, for he was running over the prairie with both of them after him. I didn't care if he ran all the way back to the Mental.

"Hughie!" King called back. "Get moving, goddamit!"

I had my breath back.

"He's turning east! What the hell is Hughie doing!"

I was vomiting.

"He's circling!"

I looked up. King was right. Bill was coming back in my direction. I got up off my knees.

"Head him back, Hughie! Get moving—out to the right! Ease up, Peter!"

My legs were shaky but I started running. Bill veered away.

"That's it! That's it! Peter keep left—Hughie right—like swings to either side! I'll be the drag and we'll herd him . . ."

"For the Mental hole!" Peter sounded almost cheerful, as though he were having a dandy time.

"Wherever he hits the river!"

That proved to be the CPR bridge, and there he tried to double back, but King closed right in on him and threw him to the ground.

We were lucky we gave Bill his bath under the CPR bridge, and if the Holy Rollers hadn't been singing at the tops of their voices when they came down to the river, we would have been in trouble. I heard them singing first, which wasn't easy with all the roaring fuss Bill was kicking up. Trying to hold him was a lot like wrestling with an egg-beater, except that an egg-beater can't practically lift you and throw you through the air. With one arm. Peter and I ended up hugging a thigh each while King had a one-arm neck lock. That freed one hand for the bar of laundry soap, but wet soap is slippery, and twice it squirted out of his grasp. The first time he managed to catch it almost before it hit the water, but the second time it got right away from him and sank out of sight.

King yelled at us to fish for it, and he put a full nelson on Bill so Peter and I could let go of his legs. I was glad to. The thrashing around had stirred up so much mud cloud it was impossible to see down there, so Peter and I had to feel around for it with one arm shoved right down and the water clear up to our ears. Even then in some places it was hard to get your fingertips to touch bottom. We should have tried to clean him up in shallower water. Peter found the soap bar. Pure luck. He stepped on it down there.

This time King said he'd keep the full nelson on, and just one of us would hold a leg while the other one soaped Bill. I grabbed the soap from Peter. That was not a very smart choice, because when I started to soap Bill's upper back and shoulders King yelled that he had already done that part and to work lower down and do his ass and his crotch. I never got to Bill's crotch, because that was when I heard the singing.

There must have been fifty of them coming from the direction of Brokenshell Grove, all strung out and aimed straight at us. They were coming quite fast, almost skipping over the prairie, their leader in a black robe and at least fifteen of them in white gowns, out in front of the others. All of them were singing. It was happy singing, almost bouncy; even at that distance you could tell they were having a lot of fun.

"Holy Rollers!" King yelled. "They're baptizing, goddamit! Under the bridge!"

It struck me as unusual that they should baptize people under a bridge.

King, of course, meant for us to get Bill and ourselves under the bridge and out of sight before it was too late. We wrestled Bill out of the river and then behind the downstream wing of the bridge's concrete footings. King threw him and pinned him. Peter and I got a tight scissors hold on each leg. King clamped a one-arm lock on his neck, but this time he kept one hand tight over Bill's mouth.

I could recognize some of the people: Fire Chief Van Wart and Mrs. Van Wart were there. For a moment I couldn't spot Irma, but that was because she wasn't wearing her red butterfly and was mixed in with the ones that had on white gowns. I hadn't known that Leon was a Holy Roller; he was wearing a black gown and was lining up the ones in white at the river edge; with his black wig he put you in mind of an

important crow. Also there was Charlie Spinks and Herb
Noseworthy, that drove the dray for Aitken's Coal and Wood,
and Mr. Plucker, Sir Walter Raleigh School janitor, and his
wife. There were others I hadn't known to be Holy Rollers. It
was as though Holy Rollers wanted to keep it secret that they
were Holy Rollers. Except for Irma Van Wart.

They were still singing, but it wasn't as though they'd
arranged ahead of time to sing certain hymns out of a hymn
book, or that the minister had told them to sing hymn
number so and so. It was just as though when they'd finished
one hymn somebody had another favorite one and started it
up, and the others all joined in.

The man in the black robe who had led them over the
prairie to the river, the fat one with red ginger hair fanned
out at the sides and back like a halo, stepped out into the
water and lifted up his robe. He gathered it in front of
himself to stuff it down into the top of his pants, which must
have had a very high waist. Then I realized that under his
robes he was wearing canvas chest waders, just as though he
were going out into a slough in fall to knock down ducks out
of a morning or evening flight. When the water reached just
above his hips he settled his feet into the mud and turned
toward the river bank.

Leon led one of the women in a white gown to the water
and then walked her out to the minister, who lifted his arm
and held it out for her to take. He put his right hand to the
nape of her neck and he said something we couldn't hear and
then he seemed to test his footing just before he threw his
arm up and back and down to plunge the woman under
water. That is not a good way to do it—with your face tipped
so the Little Souris flows right up your nose. After a count of
about three he brought her back up again, choking and
coughing, her hair streaming. She let go his arm and put both
hands up and drew them down her eyes and her nose and her
mouth. She pushed back the hair plastered across her cheeks
and turned away to go back to the river bank. She passed
Leon leading another one out to the minister to be thrown
under again.

When the first one waded out and up onto the river bank
you could see her baptizing-gown was just like a cotton
bathing-suit, the way it had sucked in to her crotch and her
belly button and the crack of her buttocks. Her breasts were

sculpted; her nipples were standing at attention. Irma was the third one submerged, and after her, skinny as a wading heron, came a man who must have found it an emotionally uplifting experience.

About then King lost his grip on Bill's mouth. Bill yelled and thrashed one leg free. Mine. He got Peter in the forehead with a heel and Peter let go and King needed both hands to get Bill under control again. It wasn't until Peter and I had a good hold on his legs again that King could get a hand over Bill's mouth to cork off the yelling.

The Holy Rollers didn't even notice. They'd got down to the last three yet to be baptized. Three or four. The preacher had one. There were two on the bank—but there was one white gown too many. The extra one was up to his hips in the water against the far bank, his face turned up to the sun, his arms outstretched with palms pleading. Blind Jesus must have got away from Buffalo Billy, but he wasn't in any danger because he had stepped into the water downstream from the preacher, where the Little Souris shallows out and isn't over your head even in the very middle. Blind Jesus angled upstream as he crossed, but the water crept up only to his chest and then receded. He missed the preacher, but he stepped out right in front of the congregation on the river bank. He kept right on going with his arms out and his head tilted to the sun, right through the singing and the praying, the dry and the dripping.

"Hallelujah!"

"Praise Him!"

"Praise God!"

"He has come again!"

"Oh, praise His Holy Name!"

They fell back and they separated as he kept on going right through them. A couple fell to their knees, then another, then the whole works. Some had their hands up in front of their chests, praying; some had their arms stretched up to him; some were shouting; some were singing; some had flopped right out on the ground and were writhing and wriggling like garter-snakes. Blind Jesus just kept right on going out over the prairie towards the late afternoon sun.

Buffalo Billy had reined up on the opposite bank; he sized up the situation; he plunged off into the water and forded the river at full gallop, kicking up spray all the way.

Afterwards, when the preacher and all the Holy Rollers had left for their Brokenshell Grove camp, and we had finished cleaning Bill up and taken him back to the cave, I said to Peter and King, "I don't think most of them ever noticed Buffalo Billy."

"You're probably right," King said. "All they saw was their miracle."

"That was no miracle," Peter said.

"Oh yes."

"It was not," Peter said.

"Yes it was."

"Just Blind Jesus," I said.

King looked at us for a minute. "Don't you fellows believe in miracles?"

"Not really," Peter said.

"Hughie?" Now King was looking just at me. "Hughie?"

It wasn't something I could answer right away. "Not that one, I don't."

He didn't let me get away with it. "You believe in miracles?"

"That was just Blind Jesus," I said.

"That does not answer my question, Hughie. I did not ask you if—just south of the CPR bridge—you believe there took place a miraculous second coming of Jesus Christ who appeared before the South Saskatchewan Holy Rollers. I asked you . . ."

"Bloody well didn't!" Peter said.

"Hmh. Not likely any miracles are going to be wasted on you fellows."

"Horse shit!"

"You watch it, Hughie!"

"Horse shit!" I don't know why I felt that angry. It always annoyed me when somebody teased me—an older kid or an adult. Especially if they grinned while they did it. King was grinning at me. What I was feeling now was much more than annoyance.

"Crazy Blind Jesus out of the Mental! Suppose it had been Horny Harold showed up—I suppose you'd call that a miracle! A Horny Harold miracle!"

"No."

"Jesus did."

"All right then!"

"But—Horny Harold didn't. Did he!"

"No."

"Jesus did."

"*Blind* Jesus!"

"*You* saw Blind Jesus—*Peter* saw Blind Jesus—*I* saw Blind Jesus—but those Holy Rollers—they saw *Jesus* Jesus."

"The hell they did!"

'Yes, they did. Right now they're all back at their Brokenshell Grove camp telling each other all about their wonderful miracle—remembering how they saw Jesus step off the opposite bank and walk across the top of the Little Souris and out among them to bless their baptism wind-up with His Holy Presence among them. . . ."

"He did not walk across any water!"

"They saw Him do it."

"They're wrong!"

"That's right. But it doesn't change the miracle. *Their* miracle."

I still felt angry. "That the way you fought the war?"

He quit grinning then. "Because you are little for your age and you wear those horn-rimmed glasses and you look with your eyes straight on a person and your face so innocent does not successfully hide the fact that—you are really—a mean little shit!" I started to feel a little better. "And I will answer your question. Yes. That is the way I fought the war. I could not have stood it or lived through it—if I hadn't fought the war that way."

"And is that the way you play hock—"

"Shut up! While you are still winning!"

I shut up. I was not angry any more.

VII

Whenever I am tolled back to that summer of 1924 I can recognize it as a special summer of defiance for Peter Deane-Cooper and me. We had King Motherwell on our side against all the other adults in their upper world. There had always been skirmishes and minor border engagements, but Bill the Sheepherder having been hidden in our prairie cave, we were now committed during those summer holidays to true war. I think Peter understood this more clearly than I did at the time.

Although we knew that we must eventually fly up there to the adult world, we knew very little of what they planned for us, had no real intelligence of their strategy. We knew who their leaders were: Judge and Mrs. Judge Hannah, Inspector and Mrs. Inspector Kydd, our Grade Four and Five and Six teacher, Louella Coldtart, the Sir Walter Raleigh Principal, Mr. Mackey, and down in the family trenches, our own parents, of course. They were as uninformed about us as we were about them. They thought they knew us, but they did not, though Mr. Mackey may have been an exception to this ignorance. On the other hand, he might not have been; we *thought* he knew, which was just about the same thing.

All that ever came down to us was the sound of thunder far above, an occasional lightning flash that gave us just blinks of revelation. In this adults-versus-kids contest Musgrave played an ambiguous role; I could not make up my mind about him, whether to accept him as a neutral and our main source of information about them, or as a double agent not to be trusted at all.

He once reported to me that Mrs. Judge Hannah drank.

That was astonishing. I said that I often sat beside her when she taught us Sunday school in Knox Presbyterian basement and that I never smelled anything off her. He said all Presbyterians drank just as much as Anglicans or even Catholics, except that Presbyterians didn't drink at all on the Sabbath, whereas Catholics laid off until after noon mass, then thought they could get away with anything they wanted to the rest of the week if they went to confession. I said that didn't prove Mrs. Judge Hannah drank and he had no way of knowing, because the Hannahs never let anybody ride in their car, let alone come inside their house to find out if Mrs. Judge Hannah drank.

I did not believe Musgrave at the time, but about a month later I carried a May Day basket to the Hannah house. Pessimistically. I had made it with flour paste from one of the wallpaper roll ends stacked in the billiard-room closet and filled it with crocuses.

I knew she was home because their long, black McLaughlin was in front of the house. I twisted the front-door bell and when there was no response I went around to the back and knocked on the screen. The inside door had been left open, which was unusual of the Hannahs, even though it was the first of May. The Saturday morning had a crystal quality about it, with all the spring sounds, from bluebottles to sparrows, magnified. I heard a stirring of life within, just at hearing pitch. Then I heard an edgeless thumping sound like some large body bumping against some piece of upholstered furniture, then the sound of slippers slapping linoleum.

She loomed in the doorway. She was wearing a wrapper and her hair was not caught up properly and she seemed confused, and Musgrave was right. She looked down at me from under her black, Calvinist eyebrows that almost met at the centre of her forehead, and I knew I had made an embarrassing, wrong decision in knocking on their screen. I handed up the May basket to her and she took it from me and she stared down at its cargo of crocuses. For a moment I thought she intended to speak, but instead she turned away. I did too.

I heard a hoarse sound from within the kitchen. I stopped halfway down the back step; it could have been crying. The screen pushed open and she was in the doorway again. She was holding out her hand to me.

There was a whole quarter in it!

The Hannahs kept pretty well to themselves, and their son Angus led, in the words of the old Scottish stonemason, a life that was "plumb but barely so." Angus was their only son, and we were lucky that Judge and Mrs. Judge Hannah were not blessed with a daughter or we would have had another flinger in our town, which already had a fair supply of them, though nothing like the mother lode of them in the old country. Angus did not play the bagpipes, but he always showed up on stage or at Sunday school in kilts with a cockerty bonnet and a turkey feather.

When we were fourteen, Angus confided in us that he intended to become Prime Minister of Canada when he grew up. Though we did not laugh at him for it, we did not take it seriously. Perhaps we should have, for he did not possess one stitch of a sense of humour and he had started practising at the age of four to become Prime Minister, by orating heroic pieces like "Incident in a French Camp," in which a young soldier brought victorious battle news to Napoleon in our Grade Seven Reader. That recitation had a snapper at the end when the fellow got the dispatch out and then dropped dead at Napoleon's feet without letting anyone know he had been mortally wounded, thus denying himself the first aid that might have kept him from hemorrhaging to death. King Motherwell said it was horse shit.

Most of the time, however, Angus declaimed his favorite "Robert Bruce and the Spider," which I didn't have to have King tell me was horse shit, because I had observed Canadian spiders a great deal, and unless Scottish spiders were a lot different from them, I knew they gave up long before Angus had made it to the end of "Robert Bruce and the Spider."

For comic relief sometimes he would do the one about King Alfred letting that peasant woman's bannocks burn when she went out to milk. Not often enough, though. And it wasn't all that funny.

The hymns Mrs, Judge Hannah picked out for us to sing in Sunday school were quite heroic and warlike: "Dare To Be a Daniel" and "Onward, Christian Soldiers" were her two favorites. As soon as we started British History in the green book, and I saw Queen Boadicea with those sickle blades attached to the hubs of her chariot wheels, I knew who Mrs. Judge Hannah reminded me of, and why being in her pres-

ence made me think of wearing shin guards; though I knew
bloody well Boadicea was not Scottish and did not drink—to
my knowledge. Or to Musgrave's.

My major adversary in this on-going war was my own
mother, of course. She could have been an eminent Victorian;
indeed she was one—in our town. "Our girl never goes
covered-wagon," my father once said to me. "Calling-cards
and hallmarked sterling and Royal Crown Derby all the way."
He was not kidding about those calling-cards. He had printed
them for her himself. It was too bad she didn't have any blind
friends, for with your fingertips you could feel her name
raised like Braille in script type on them. I think my father
did them without telling her and brought home a whole box
and gave them to her with a straight face. She was delighted
with them; from then on she sprayed them all over town, so
the joke had backfired on him. Before that year was out my
father kept getting calling-card orders from other ladies in
town, who wanted to leave them on little silver dishes just
inside front doors of ladies who were not home.

My mother spent always some part of her day at the
varnished oak desk with skinny legs in the music room,
dipping her pen and scratching notes on her own deckled
sheets of writing paper my father had monogrammed for her.
My mother sent a lot of notes to people: to our minister, Mr.
Rosscamp, to the ladies in her Burning Bush booth or the
Kitchener of Khartoum Chapter of the IODE, to people who
were having birthdays or babies or weddings or funerals or
graduations. For delivery of these notes she relied about
equally on me and the Royal Mail.

When I needed an absence excuse for school, she folded
her note always in the same way, eight times in on itself till it
became a long, white ribbon, then down from each end in
two slant creases to make a double, geometrical boomerang.
These notes did not start out "My Dear Miss Coldtart:" or
"My Dear Mr. Mackey:"; they didn't even start out "Dear . . .";
just "Miss Coldtart:" and "Mr. Mackey:" followed by the raw
command: "Excuse Hughie for his absence from school Thursday." Below that: "and oblige." These were not arrogant
notes; they were simply written with the conviction that if
she had taken the trouble to write them and fold them
carefully into white boomerangs, there was no need for
explanation or justification. Neither Miss Coldtart nor Mr.

Mackey ever questioned these paper absolutes. As King Motherwell would say, they were pretty strong medicine.

My mother would as soon go out in public without her bloomers on as without a hat or gloves. Yet this was the same woman who painted all the upstairs floor by herself because Hertha was so careless, combing the fake oak grain into the base coat before varnishing it. She was also a self-taught paper-hanger, who had done every room in our house except the kitchen.

My mother and I most often clashed over my glasses, right from the time she took me into Mr. Bradley's shop to buy my first pair at the age of five. Mr. Bradley fitted me with very large and horn-rimmed ones so that I must have looked like a ground owl in a middy suit and sailor hat. He told my mother that I had a lazy left eye which, if not corrected now, would get much worse; he was quite successful in explaining to people why they should buy glasses from him, and would not be happy until he had fitted them on every single weaned child in our district. When my mother took me out of Mr. Bradley's and down the street to the print shop to show my father, he laughed as soon as he saw me.

I cried. My father hugged me and said he was sorry for laughing, and took me into Chan Kai's and bought me a strawberry ice-cream cone. The next day I flushed the glasses down the upstairs toilet. Unintentionally.

I went through about four pair a year after that, which annoyed my mother, who kept reminding me that Morton Hepworth, who lived on the south side of town, was still wearing the original pair his mother had got for him from Mr. Bradley over five years before. Mr. Bradley must have got to Morton Hepworth while he was still crawling. Even if Morton had lived on our side or town, he would never have been any friend of mine.

My glasses jumped off me and got stepped on; Fat Isbister smashed at least three pair; I would leave them with my clothes on the bank of the Little Souris and come out and forget them and not be able to find them when I remembered and went back for them; I dived into the river with them still on and they got drowned. Sometimes I simply lost them. I could not tell the difference in my seeing when they were on and when they were off, and I told my mother this many times. If I could see just as well without them, probably I didn't need them any more. My mother said she did not need a cross-eyed son, either!

My first year in university I would stop wearing them, until thirty years later when the print got smaller in telephone directories and on medicine bottles. I am not cross-eyed yet.

Other adults to worry about were Inspector Kydd and Mrs. Inspector Kydd. Until the year we hid Bill the Sheepherder in our cave, I generally saw them when they were riding down Sixth on their way to the prairie beyond. They were always followed by their Russian wolfhounds, with long and aristocratic noses, pure and gaunt, canine arcs, most often with their tails sucked up under their bellies like inverted commas. With these dogs the Kydds hunted coyotes.

Both horses were black. Mrs. Inspector Kydd rode hers side-saddle—a stud. He had black knackers under him the size of tennis balls, and held by the spell of erotic fantasy, which seemed to be always, he would lower a fifth leg with an end on it like a giant black toadstool. Three feet long at least. Whenever they rode out Sixth to chase coyotes, the Kydds often stopped in front of our house, just the right distance away from theirs to dismount and tighten the girths on their horses. Mrs. Inspector Kydd did her own, and I once saw her rap her horse's erection with her riding-crop. One leg flinched up; that long, licorice whang sucked back elastic-quick, fast as a middy-waist garter up your pant leg, and hell just about went out for recess for that poor stud after she corrected him that way, but she handled him by herself and climbed back up. One of the Kydd Russian wolfhounds was stubbornly horny too, though you didn't often get a good look at his long, carrot erection, the way it was covered most of the time by the plume tail sucked up under his belly.

That year Mrs. Inspector Kydd began to come to our house to have tea with my mother. Several times a week. Her first name was Diana. I now knew that, because my mother began saying to my father and me, "Diana said this..." or "Diana said that..." all the time. Like Peter's mother, she was English, but they did not talk quite the same, nor did they laugh alike, either. Peter's mother had a long and crystal laugh that began up high and slid down the scale to hit bottom with: "Haow loveleh!" Mrs. Inspector Kydd barked. Usually three times. When she laughed.

Like Bill the Sheepherder, and King, Inspector Kydd was a war veteran too, the Boer War into the bargain. It was hard for me to be sure which side he had fought for in the Great War, because if you switched his Mountie hat for a spiked helmet, he would be a doppelgänger for Kaiser Bill. He scared the hell out of me. Especially the summer of 1924. He was, after all, in charge of the search for Bill the Sheepherder, and their house was just two doors down from the Deane-Coopers'. Every time I had to pass the Mounted Police house to visit Peter, or saw the Kydds riding down the street with their three Russian wolfhounds behind them, my heart stumbled. I wished she'd just go drink her tea with somebody else. I avoided the Mounted Police house as well as I could that summer while we had Bill in our cave. But my mother wasn't making it easy for me, the way she kept sending me over there on errands for her now that she and Diana were so thick with each other. Inside the Kydd front hallway I had noticed a large plate-glass case, a lot like an aquarium without goldfish. Inside on a green velvet pad lay what looked like a wooden potato-masher, except that it was split in half and hinged at the bulb end. I knew it wasn't a potato-masher, because why the hell would anybody keep a split potato-masher in an empty aquarium in their front hallway? The day my mother needed her Royal Crown Derby cake plate with the cover back for her Burning Bush booth tea, and she trusted me to get it and bring it home, Mrs. Inspector Kydd told me what was in the plate-glass case in their front hallway.

It was a lemon-squeezer!

I did not say to her, "Why the hell do you keep a lemon-squeezer in a plate-glass case in your front hallway?" because I guessed it had to be a pretty important lemon-squeezer. I was right indeed. Mrs. Inspector Kydd's father had been personal surgeon to "Sir Charles Dickens," she explained to me, and this was "Sir Charles Dickens'" own personal lemon-squeezer, given by "Sir Charles Dickens" to her father out of gratitude for treatment of chronic quinsy and a double rupture. I had no reason to doubt her. Bill Sykes could have brained Nancy with it.

Even though she was turning out to be the most interesting of my mother's friends, the less I saw of Mrs. Inspector

Kydd that summer, the better. But it was difficult to avoid her if she and my mother liked each other so much that they kept having tea. Whether I came in the back door or the front door I could tell just as soon as I stepped inside our house that she was there. She was the only one of my mother's friends who smoked. Her cigarettes were long, black ones and she smoked them in a silver cigarette-holder that telescoped. They did not smell roast-lovely like King's Millbanks or my father's cigars. They smelled like mare's urine.

As soon as she'd see me, she'd bark as though my appearance was surprisingly funny. She said things there could be no answer for, like: "Oh, there you are."

My mother would say, "Say hello to Mrs. Kydd, Hughie."

I would say, "Hello, Mrs. Kydd."

Almost every time the next thing she'd say would be, "Aren't you the lucky boy."

Now just how the hell do you answer that one? "Am I?" or "Do you really think so?" or "No—I'm not." or "Why am I?"

"Having such a lovely mother," was the right answer.

Some of the time my mother was all right, but actually what Mrs. Inspector Kydd meant was that my mother was lovely-*looking*, because one time she said, "Having such a *handsome* mother."

Even though my mother's first name was Helen, as a child I never thought her face was likely to launch a thousand ships. But she certainly imprinted me, for in later years few blondes would even light up candles inside me, while dark eyes and hair and cream skin often did. I realize now that Mrs. Inspector Kydd was right: my mother was Gibson Girl beautiful. She looked like the long heroines illustrated in the awful books she read, particularly the one with her hair done up like the top of a round loaf of bread, in The *Husbands of Helen*. My mother was quite vain about her hair, her skin, her waist. Also it was pretty obvious to Mrs. Inspector Kydd or anyone else that I had not been a bottle-fed baby. What was not so obvious to somebody outside our family, which included Hertha, was that my mother was as tough as corset whalebone and had two voices: her social performance voice, and the one she used every day on us. I guess she had a third voice, too, for when she sang, it came out a plum-rich alto.

Either at our piano or in Knox Presbyterian choir she could sing to beat hell, and for that my father and I were proud of her.

On second thought, I loved her, too.

An awful thought occurred to me that maybe Inspector Kydd might be sending his wife over to our place just to check up on me because he had suspicions that somehow I was involved with Bill the Sheepherder. Since the Kydds lived just two doors from Peter, she might have reported to Inspector Kydd that Peter and I must be up to something, judging from the number of times I visited the Deane-Cooper house. Through the window she could have easily seen Peter and me the time we lugged half the Deane-Cooper pantry down the street, or else Mrs. Deane-Cooper could have complained to her that she was missing marmalade and dairy butter, preserves and tea and sugar and canned milk. Peter said I was being ridiculous, and don't get the wind up so.

I told myself that Peter was right and my fear died down some, only to flare up again when, instead of "Well, there you are," Mrs. Inspector Kydd said, "Seeing a great deal of Deane-Cooper Minor this summer, aren't we now?" I knew just how that stud felt when she got him a good one with her riding-crop. "Regular David and Jonathan, eh?" Then she barked.

That was late July, and it was a week after that I came in for a peanut-butter sandwich and found the tea-wagon overturned in the archway, then heard my mother in the music room. She was on the cherry settee there under Brahms, Bach, Beethoven, Handel, Liszt, and Mozart, and one whole side of her black hair hung down her cheek. She was crying. I asked her what was the matter, but she just shook her head, and got up, and I followed her out of the music room and to the foot of the stairs. I asked her again why was she crying and she said never mind, and then she said please don't say anything to your father.

After she came downstairs with her hair done up but her eyes still red, she set the tea-wagon back up and began to pick up cups and plates and sandwiches. When I went to help her she said, never mind, she'd do it herself, and just go outside and play.

That night when my father got home from the shop she

seemed fine. I did not say anything to him about the tea-wagon.

I felt relieved; I wouldn't have to worry about Mrs. Inspector Kydd so much if there'd been a fight. It must have been a dandy to tip over our tea-wagon.

My mother never sent me over to the Mounted Police house after that, nor did Mrs. Inspector Kydd come to our house again. I hoped the only time I would see her would be when they rode by with their three thin, Russian ghosts.

I underestimated Mrs. Inspector Kydd. A week later I saw her in a Blue Bird Cafe booth. She could have still been trying to find out about Bill the Sheepherder because she was having a soda with Bella Motherwell.

I asked Peter shouldn't we tell King about it, and this time Peter didn't say I was being ridiculous. He said wait and see, and let's keep an eye on both of them. I saw them together in the Blue Bird three times that summer. Peter also saw Mrs. Inspector Kydd going into the Walker Block once. I saw her go in three times. After the second time I said maybe we should tell King now, but Peter said he didn't think we should. He couldn't seem to give me any reason for not telling King about it. I also saw Mrs. Inspector Kydd with Bella in Firmstone's Department Store. In the Ladies' Dresses Department.

If Mrs. Inspector Kydd ever picked a fight with Bella it would be a better match than the one with my mother, because Bella had been tough from birth.

I knew this because I heard Dr. Sinclair once telling my father how he delivered Dan Spragget's hired girl of a baby in the spring of 1904. He'd got out there late and Bella began to come on the black leather of his brandnew buggy, and he got her mother back into the shack and up onto the kitchen table just in time.

"Slippery little thing squirted right out of my hands and skidded off the oilcloth—bounced onto the dirt floor. I got her and the mother out to the buggy and picked up the reins and then I remembered the placenta and I went back inside to look for it. Under the table—the stove—the woodbox—in the coal-scuttle. It wasn't anywhere in there. I covered every inch of the ground between the back door and the buggy. Dan all the time had been seeding—just going round and round that field next to the shack with the drill—didn't pull those horses up or climb down once to see what was going on. I stopped him the next time round. He said, 'What the hell's a plah-sent-yah?' I said, 'Afterbirth.' He said, 'Maybe she et it.' I said, 'Goddamit, man, this is serious!' He said, 'So's spring seedin' an' I'm just tryin' to make a helpful suggestion an' she could have seen it an' dragged if off somewheres. She'll eat anything.' I realized then he meant his dog, not his hired girl. I said, 'Did you see the dog with anything?' He said, 'Just a gopher and that was this morning about nine o'clock. I ain't even seen the goddam bitch since then.'"

Bella had survived that.

"Turned out to be a real beauty," Dr. Sinclair said. My father agreed with him. So did I. Bella always made me think of a gipsy girl, because her eyes were black as tar and she didn't do her hair up in cootie-catchers or have it bobbed, just left it hanging free. Her skin was paraffin white like the candles we lighted our caves with. She had a scar like a seam from the right side of her nose down to just below the corner of her mouth, but it didn't stop her from looking Proserpine-lovely. I got that out of my *Golden Book of Legends*.

She had worked as a maid a few places around town and then in the Blue Bird Cafe before she married King. Even if King had told her about the way we had Bill the Sheepherder in our cave, I knew she wouldn't squeal on us to Mrs. Inspector Kydd. Peter agreed with me. I still thought I'd better keep an eye on both of them.

VIII

I did not keep count of the number of fits Bill the Sheepherder took while he was in our cave. Peter saw him have two of them before I saw my first one, and that was good enough for me. Being in on the first time that King had to give Bill a needle was bad enough.

"The needle's for being crazy," King explained. "Those fits are a different thing altogether. No way of predicting a seizure—and the medicine for it doesn't seem to ease his fit all that much. He's just got to ride them out on his own. With the other—at least the needle can keep him from hurting himself too much when he goes off the end of the spring-board. I'll keep a pretty regular check on him—and I can tell pretty well ahead of time when he's due."

All the same, King wasn't ready for the first time. We always left the car well back from the cave and the homesteader shack and walked the rest of the way, and three mornings after the second coming of Christ to the South Saskatchewan Holy Rollers, which made it a Wednesday, Peter and I and King heard Bill when we were still a good hundred yards from the cave. He was well into his torment and roaring underground, and he must have been throwing himself about pretty violently, because you'd swear the sod was lifting and settling over the cave roof. If he was doing it with his head, you'd think he'd brain himself on the boards, or else that dry old shiplap brittle off the homesteader shack might crack and give way, and two tons of dirt come down on him and smother him to death.

King ran back for the car. With his medical bag he crouched down at the tunnel mouth, got out the medicine

97

bottle and the syringe and loaded it, and then started into the tunnel. Head first. Then right away he came back out and switched ends so he'd be going down in there feet first.

Bill got really wild. I don't think any rogue elephant ever kicked up more fuss. King was yelling, too.

King came back out. Head first.

"Jesus! For a minute there—I didn't know who was giving who a needle!"

"What do we do now!" I said.

"Now—we wait."

"What for, sir?"

"Needle to take hold."

"How long for it to take hold?" I said.

"Couple minutes."

Five minutes later Bill was still going strong, and he started to come out of the cave to get at us. King dropped down and got a foot on Bill's shoulder and another on his face and shoved him back down, and then turned and plugged off the tunnel opening with his ass.

King shook his head. "God, I gave him at least a double dose—should have taken care of two of him by now!"

"Perhaps you got a bad batch, sir."

But it hadn't been, because Bill was softening down. Then all was quiet in the cave.

King got up.

"Is he always going to be this bad?" I said.

"Prognosis isn't too good," King said. "We'll just have to wait and see." He was looking down at the cave. Thoughtfully. He seemed to make up his mind. "I got an idea. Come on with me."

"Where to, sir?"

"We just might—do a little—rustling."

"Rustling!" Peter forgot to say "sir."

"Mmm-hmh."

"Rustling what?" I said.

"Sheep."

"What the hell for?" I said.

"For Bill. Sheepherder, isn't he? Lived with sheep most of his life—excepting during his war years—and being in the army isn't all that different from joining up with a herd of sheep."

Fat Isbister once told me a dirty story about a hired man and a ewe, but I knew that wasn't what King had in mind for Bill.

"Seems to me there was some slaughter going on over there. Second thought—I'll handle it alone. You fellows go have a swim or something."

"What about Bill?" I said.

"He won't be waking up much before supper-time."

As we walked towards the Little Souris, Peter said he wouldn't have minded helping King to rustle a sheep out of Muhlbiers' herd, and I said it was all right with me if King wanted to do it by himself.

"But just how would a sheep help Bill?" Peter said.

"Search me," I said.

"Still, I'm jolly sure King knows what he's doing."

Thinking about Bill raging and roaring and thumping around down in our cave and scaring the hell out of me, and King spearing needles into him, and everybody searching for him and dragging the river for him, I wasn't so goddam sure King knew what he was doing.

"King is the pluckiest man I've ever known."

And what would they do to Peter and me when they found out we'd been hiding an escaped, dangerous mental patient in our cave all along—if he didn't get hold of us first, and beat us or strangle us to death! I wasn't so sure now that King had let us make our own decision to keep Bill down there in the first place. I did not say any of this to Peter as we walked towards the Mental hole.

We never got there. A coyote scalded past us with his brush lined out and his belly to the ground. He was in some hurry because one of the Kydds' Russian wolfhounds had his long nose practically right up that coyote's ass-hole. A moment later came the other two hounds and then Mrs. Inspector Kydd drumming the black stud with her riding-crop, straight up and comfortable as though she were seated side-saddle on a trochaic toilet bowl. A good hundred yards behind came Inspector Kydd. Neither the dogs nor the coyote nor the Kydds seemed to notice Peter and me. They were carrying the good news from Ghent to Aix. All six.

"We must go back!" Peter said. "Warn King!"

"They're after that coyote—not King!"

"What if they catch him rustling Muhlbiers' sheep!"

"They aren't going to. He can hear them coming a mile off. Let's go to the CPR hole, though."

"They don't hang people any more for sheep-rustling, do they?" Peter asked while we were undressing.

"Not lately." I now knew one way Peter could annoy me; that was by seeming to enjoy trouble and having the gizzard scared out of you. The worse it was, the more he enjoyed it.

"But I still don't understand it—why ever does he want a sheep? What possible good could it do for Bill?"

"He's going to offer it up—as a burnt sacrifice."

"Really! Oh—now I see—like a Red Indian medicine man might do."

Another thing about Peter: he was not all that swift at recognizing sarcasm.

We had just got into the water when we heard the hounds again and got under the bridge. We were in for another nasty shock, because that coyote was headed straight for our bridge and he hit it with about the speed of a CPR silk freight, the first Russian wolfhound just a quarter of a length behind him. At the other end of the bridge the coyote had the hound by at least ten full lengths and then by everything, because one of the hound's front feet went through the trestle ties and he pretty well gave up the chase right there.

That was one smart coyote!

On her black stud Mrs. Inspector Kydd veered away from the bridge approach and took the left bank of the Little Souris, forded the river as easy as Buffalo Billy, came out on the other side, and that was the last we saw of her. But not Inspector Kydd, whose horse balked in full gallop at the near side of the bridge and lobbed the Inspector into the river.

Inspector Kydd didn't even see Peter and me up to our necks under the bridge. He stood up dripping in about a foot of water, and as he walked out and up onto the bridge he was unbuttoning the flap on his RCMP pistol holster; a minute later we heard a shot. The hound's crying quit.

Inspector Kydd laid the white body over the front of his saddle and climbed up to ride back the way he'd come. I supposed he would make a stop at the town garbage dump.

While we were dressing, Peter said wouldn't it be simply great if they crossed a prairie wolf with a wolfhound.

"Think they could mate—what a great mix you'd get then! Wild and tame!"

"Won't work."

"Oh—fail to fertilize her then."

"He's got to catch her first."

"I see what you mean," Peter said.

The rest of that summer and fall the Kydds were followed by only two Russian wolfhounds whenever they went out after coyotes. I rather hoped they never did get the one that lured the wolfhound over the bridge and to his doom, though I had no way of telling. I was pretty sure the hound Inspector Kydd had to destroy was the horny one.

The next day we learned why King had wanted a sheep for Bill. Peter and I found them all inside the homesteader shack, with Bill sitting as quiet as you please in there, on a backless kitchen chair King must have brought out. By the time we got there, King had already shaved Bill and was giving him a haircut. Bill had a little lamb cradled in his lap.

It was a bum lamb King had remembered seeing, rejected or orphaned by its mother. It was sucking on the nippled beer bottle Bill was holding to its mouth.

A couple of days later Peter and I called in at the Royal Pool Hall and King drove us out to the cave. He had thrown a short-handled trench shovel and a rake and hoe in the back of the McLaughlin.

"Something we got to do," King said as we passed the Fairgrounds, then turned off Government Road and onto the prairie. "We got to wash him off again."

"Again!"

"Why?" Peter said.

"Partly his fault—partly ours. After our close call with the Holy Rollers we just slapped those filthy clothes back on him without washing *them*—put him into the cave without cleaning it out."

"He isn't going to like it," Peter said.

"We'll see."

We didn't have to smoke him out this time.

As always, he was underground when we got there.

King bent over the tunnel entrance at the rosebush "Come on out, Bill!"

He turned to Peter. "Get that trench shovel and rake and hoe. We're going to clean out the cave as well."

Bill's head had appeared in the tunnel opening. "Up out of there." Bill came half-way out. "Going for a ride." Bill came out a little more. "And another swim." Bill tried to duck back down inside but King got him by the back or his shirt. There wasn't any struggle. Bill came all the way out and stood up.

He was surprisingly co-operative as he climbed into the front seat beside King. No fuss at all clear to the CPR bridge. It was just as though going for a ride and a swim had been his idea in the first place. He let King take off his shoes for him, but he unbuttoned his shirt and pants himself. He climbed out of his underwear all by himself too, and then took the bar of laundry soap King held out to him. He soaped himself all over, then waded out and lowered himself several times to rinse off.

Peter and I rubbed and scrubbed his socks and underwear and shirt and pants, then hung them up on the railroad trestle to dry in the sun.

All of us went in for a swim then. Bill just sat in the shallow water under the bridge where King led him and told him to stay out of sight. He watched us while we made the moon rise and ducked each other and walked on our hands. It's simple to walk on your hands with most of you under water. King made a stirrup and threw Peter and me high in the air for back dives and somersaults. When I came to the surface after my second one I looked over to Bill. For the first time ever since he'd hidden in our cave, he was grinning.

We left before his clothes were completely dry, but King said that was all right; we'd better head back while our luck was still holding out. After we'd all dressed, King took the bottle down from the trestle. He didn't put it back right away. He held it out to Bill. That was the second time I'd ever seen Bill grin. From ear to ear.

When King said we'd all take turns at cleaning the cave, I volunteered to go first. That way I'd be working mostly on the tunnel. I wouldn't have to go very far inside, and most of the time I'd be the distance of the rake or hoe handle away from the stuff I was pulling out. Even so, when I kneeled down at the entrance hole to shove the rake in, I got a full breath of what was inside. I felt like throwing up. I pulled back and stood to get some fresh air.

King said. "You feeling all right?"

"In a minute."

It was hard to believe that in less than two weeks a human being could leave all the garbage there was in there: blue bread-crusts and apple cores, pork-chop and prairie-chicken bones, condensed-milk cans, carrot- and turnip- and beet-tops and corn-cobs. There were little tin spades and hearts and clubs off his chewing-tobacco plugs. Bill must have gone through a plug a day; it was lucky for him that King ran the Royal Pool Hall and could keep him supplied in wholesale quantity. Mostly, though, there were sheep turds from the little orphan lamb. He kept it down there with him all the time. He slept with it.

King did the worst of it; he took the trench shovel inside with him and dug a whole new floor in there, throwing the dirt into the tunnel for me and Peter to pull the rest of the way out.

We burned what we could and buried the rest. King said to Bill, "Keep it like that. I'm leaving you the trench shovel. You bury everything—and put the sods back over the way we did."

Just before we left I said to King, "Could I hold the little lamb?"

"Ask Bill," King said. "It's his."

Bill was giving it another beer bottle of canned milk, and I didn't know exactly how to get through to him about holding his little lamb.

"Bill?"

He looked up at me.

I held out my hand towards the lamb. "Can I hold him?"

Bill's face darkened and he clutched the lamb tighter and turned away. Then he turned back again and looked down at it with its flop ears like an umbrella and he looked back up at me and then he pulled the nipple out of the lamb's mouth and it struggled to find it again. It bleated. Bill handed up the beer bottle to me.

Then the lamb.

The lamb's eyes were like blue almonds with clouds in them. He slurped. And I knew why "The Ninety and Nine" would always be my favorite hymn.

Bill wouldn't let Peter hold his lamb.

That night I took my bath. I don't suppose I ever had one that my mother didn't come into my bedroom after to hug me and kiss me and say, "That's my lovely clean smelling son."

This time she said, "That's my—what is that smell?"

Sheep smell hangs right onto you. "What smell?"

She sniffed. "I can't place it—quite." She sniffed again. "Hughie?"

"I can't smell anything."

She leaned down over me again. "You been in the publishing office?"

I said, "Oh—that smell."

It seemed to satisfy her. She might not have been able to identify the smell of sheep lanolin, but in all the years she'd slept with my father she must have become pretty familiar with printer's ink. It has an oily smell with a bitter edge to it, and doesn't give up in a hurry, either.

IX

After almost three weeks together, both Bill and the orphan lamb were doing just fine, except for Bill's convulsions. Both were putting on weight so that Bill no longer looked so much like a skinny sheep as a fat one, and the lamb was no longer a lamb any more. Sheep seemed to grow so much faster than colts or pups or kittens. Or me.

"Must be getting pretty tight quarters for the both of you down there," King said to Bill. "Better leave him outside."

Bill didn't object very much, though the sheep did for a while. Above or underground, the sheep wanted to stay close to Bill.

All the same, having Bill in our cave was not getting any easier for me; the fabric of lies, pretence, and dissemblance was getting more and more complicated. I think we could have robbed the Home Bank more simply; once that job was pulled, I'm sure you'd have to be extremely careful, but you wouldn't be called on for the invention and practice of so many intricate and believable fictions. You wouldn't have to explain the unexplainable nearly so frequently: regular absences from home, and for long periods of time. It was more like robbing a bank over and over again.

When you were asked where you'd been all this time, you could say, "I went out onto the prairie." But raw answers like that would do only for a few times, then they had to be adorned. You had better have a reason ready for being out there, or you'd find yourself asked for one when you weren't set for it.

"What were you doing out there?"

"Drowning out gophers."

If you hadn't been shooting from the hip you would have been ready for: "Municipality hasn't been paying tail bounties since the middle of the month."

See! "Ah—well it was Ike's idea."

"Ike didn't know they'd stopped paying for gopher tails, and you wouldn't tell him?"

"I told him, but he said we could just save them till next spring. Ike does that anyway with what he gets *after* the fifteenth of May, when they drop from three cents a tail to two cents a tail. He saves any tails he gets after the fifteenth of May to sell the next spring before the fifteenth of May so he can get three cents a tail. Instead of two. He says it works out to fifty percent more on the money you don't get from not turning them in after the fifteenth of May."

Complicated explanations were dangerous; the trick was to get them economical and right, no details unless requested. Too many proffered specifics, as most criminals and lawyers know, could make you vulnerable. It was astonishing to me to learn that summer how truth is so well rooted in actuality.

"Where have you been?"

"Out on the prairie."

"With whom?"

"Some other guys."

"What other guys?"

"Hodder—Angus—Austin.... "

"Isn't he still in quarantine?"

"Oh—I meant we went by there to ask if he could go out, but his mother said he still had to stay in his yard another week, and instead Hodder came with us."

"Hodder was in the shop to pick up the auction notices for his father."

"Then I guess he wasn't with us. There was a whole lot of us out there."

"It's after nine—where have you been?"

"Out on the prairie—south of town—by the cemetery."

Not a good answer. Just "Out on the prairie—south of town" would have been much better.

"What were you doing at the cemetery?"

"Shooting."

"Near the cemetery? You trying to kill somebody!"

"They're mostly dead out there anyway." A smart-ass answer could be the most dangerous of all, though one like that worked pretty well with my father.

"Get anything?"

"Nothing." Top marks for an answer like that, and not an easy one to give; for once you'd lied about what you'd done, you were strongly tempted to take a greater creative leap and say you'd knocked over three magpies, a prairie chicken, two jacks, a weasel—a badger—and came close on a skunk and a coyote. Only a city zoo could have been so generous with that many wild animals in one outing.

The difficult skill I had to learn that summer was to walk a defensive high wire, using as much truth as possible for my balance pole. With no life net.

"How the hell could you hit anything after dark?"

"Huh!"

"It is now twenty after nine—dusk by eight. Where the hell have you been, Hugh!"

"Oh—we came in early—then we played tag in the lumberyards. Sorry."

I don't think I ever lied to King Motherwell. Even if I had wanted to, I don't think I could have pulled it off with him. Sometimes his eyes would be quite held on your face, something the same effect as a magnifying-glass condensing down the light to a white dot that burns. Mr. Mackey had that power, but for a different reason than King: to totally frighten you. All the same, that look from King didn't make you feel exactly comfortable. With King it was as though his attention was not really present; within himself he had wandered off into another country, and he simply was not there with you. It wasn't anything you had done or said that had sent him off. Something inside himself had attracted his attention, and when he did come back to you, it was as though he was not aware that he had left you. There was no apology for leaving you. He did not know that he had been away from you at all. Even though I've never known any, I've heard that some Indians have that look.

King had been born on an Indian reserve when his father was a Methodist missionary to the Salteaux in the Moose Mountains way east of us, and somehow there should have been a long eagle feather hanging slant down the front of one ear. He didn't *look* Indian, but he walked Indian, as though he were being carried along on the soft flow of moccasins. If he'd carried a coup stick it would have seemed quite natural; he was the kind of man who'd had lots of victories.

He lived with Bella in a suite in the Walker Block, and I saw the inside of that suite a lot of times before the summer of 1924 was over. The Walker Block had been built in the boom years before the war, but for stores, not suites. It had a shallow, fan-shaped entrance with plate glass on the slant sides and along the front, too, so that people inside had to have long curtains drawn not just at night but during the day to keep people out on the street from staring in at what they were doing.

To me it seemed an unusual suite for King to live in. As soon as you stepped in the room, it blushed: pink curtains, pink cushions, pink lamp-shades, ruffled pink skirt on the end table by the mostly pink chesterfield. The lamp-shade on that end table was actually the hoop skirt of a lady with a high white wig that had dropped a long curl down the front of her ear. All the kewpie dolls were pink.

Pretty nearly every time I visited, there was the punk-stick smell of incense coming from the green Buddha sitting in the middle of the coffee table, beside a long radio set. Bella had the earphones on a lot.

"I got Chicago an' KOA an' New York last night. An' the night before, just as clear as anything—no static at all—I got San Francisco."

"You didn't have those earphones grafted on your head all night—you wouldn't sleep to noon every day. Have some time to swamp this place out—darn a few socks. Why don't you do what other women do!"

"Oh sure! Tea with Mrs. Marshall—golf with Mrs. Judge

Hannah! Daughters of the bloody Nile—Kitchener of Khartoum Chapter the IODE—all that shit!"

I think she was the only woman I ever heard say shit. They had arguments like that all the time, and you couldn't say who won. You couldn't say who lost, either.

She might not make it into the Kitchener of Khartoum Chapter of the IODE, but Mrs. Inspector Kydd would have had her hands full in a fight with her.

Another time I called in at the Walker Block so King and I could go out to the cave, and they were at it again.

"That a new dress you got on?"

"No. I had it a long time."

"I never saw it before."

"Lot you don't seem to see."

"Skirt *that* short I'd . . ."

"I shortened it."

"Hell you did! That is a new dress. You got that when I was on my last trip south, didn't you!"

"No."

"You running up bills all over town again!"

"No."

"You charge that dress?"

"No."

"Paid cash for it, did you?"

She didn't answer him.

"I said . . ."

"I heard you!"

"All right then! Where'd you get the money for that dress!"

"It's a real cheap dress."

"Strikes me that way too! Where'd you get the money for it?"

"I saved up for it."

"Out of what and how much?"

"Grocery money."

"How much?"

"I can't remember exactly."

"Try!"

"Yes, sir!"

I noticed that if you kept quiet and maybe moved off a

ways and looked down and fiddled with something, adults didn't pay so much attention to you, and you were liable to hear something interesting. It worked most of the time, except with teachers and my mother.

"Why can't you ever give a person a straight answer! Why the hell 'can't you level with a person! Just once with me!"

I was pretending I was pretty interested in that green Buddha's belly-button.

"You bought—just what you got—big shot!"

"Bought! Married!"

"So? Big difference!"

"Goddam rights there is!"

"I guess I didn't notice," Bella said.

"Well, start noticing!"

"Yes, sir! On the double, sir!"

"Stop that!"

"Left—right—ass-holes tight . . . "

"Watch it!"

" . . . foreskins to the front . . . "

"Dammit! The kid . . . "

"Kids! You want kids! You'll just have to excuse my frozen pelvis, sir, and give your baby order to the Firmstone stork! Because I can't have any—can I!"

"Bella!"

"Ever!"

"Outside, Hughie! Please!"

"I thought Dr. Sinclair explained that to us, sir!"

I got out. Even through the door behind me I heard the slap like a rifle crack. Then another one.

A minute later when he came out, I saw that the whole left side of King's face was red. He didn't say a word all the way out to the cave.

I knew about that new pink dress of hers. She hadn't charged it at Firmstone's Department Store. She hadn't saved up for it out of grocery money. I was in Infants' Wear by the bald stork with his head tipping up and down, and I saw Miss Delicate in Ladies' Wear put the money and the bill for it into the little cage that ran like a wind-up train all the way up to Mr. Firmstone on the balcony. It was Mrs. Inspector Kydd who gave Miss Delicate the cash for the pink dress.

At first when I asked my mother if I could sleep out by the Little Souris with Peter, she said no. As usual. I said why not, and she said it might storm and I said it hadn't rained since May and all the farmers were yelling drought again, and Peter had a waterproofed tarp, anyway.

"It's just that—I—it's not a good idea—two boys alone out there. . . ."

"We won't be alone. King Motherwell's going to camp with us."

I had saved that to tell her only when I needed it, for I was pretty sure King was not her first choice of someone to look after her son. It was, however, an answer to her concern about our safety out on the prairie at night.

"The night air—your chest . . ."

"I haven't coughed for over a month. We'll have a camp-fire and a groundsheet, and if you'll let me, we can use the buffalo robe." Peter loved our buffalo robe, which served as a car robe in early spring and late fall till the car was put up on blocks in the garage and the radiator drained for the winter. During the summer the robe lay on the chain swing in our back sun-porch. It scratched.

"Let me think about it."

As soon as she said that, I knew I was winning. I had been careful about my timing so that I had three days to work on her. That evening, after my father came home from the shop, I went into the den and asked him and he said, sure, he guessed it was all right with him, but to ask my mother. I said I would, then went out into the breakfast room and asked her if she had thought it over enough yet. She said she didn't think it was such a good idea.

"Peter's mother does."

"Well, you're not Peter and I'm not Peter's mother."

"But if she says it's all right for him—why isn't it all right for me?"

"Because she doesn't have to worry about Peter getting a cold that will settle on his chest and turn into bronchitis! Because Peter—because—you just got over one session!"

"That was over a month ago!" I couldn't tell her how hard I had worked at ending my quarantine after we blew Musgrave's grampa up in the backhouse.

"Peter's mother lets him do stuff all the time."

"That's her business if she wants to let her son lie out on the damp prairie—half-cooked food—eaten alive by mosquitoes."

"Mosquitoes never killed anybody yet, and we know how to build a smudge."

"I'll talk it over with your father."

"And if he says all right . . ."

"I'll talk it over with him."

"If he says yes, then can I . . ."

"We'll see."

"If you're not going to let me go, then there isn't any reason for you to talk it over with him. Is there?"

"We'll see."

From her voice I knew that was the end of that round.

They must have talked about it in bed because she was angry at breakfast the next morning.

"How many times have I told you not to sneak behind my back to your father!"

"I didn't sneak. . . ."

"Yes, you did—you did not say a word last night to me that you'd asked him! You did not say a word to him that you had asked me first!"

"You never asked me if I asked him!"

"I shouldn't have had to! Now—you ask me again if you can spend the night sleeping out on the prairie with Peter! Ask me!"

"Can I?"

"No!"

This was why I had been so careful of my timing. I needed two days at least during which I would not bring the matter up with her or with my father. I would speak only when either of them spoke to me; I would not go outside the house; I would be consistently sad, as I had been when I was trying to get her to break my quarantine. But this time with a difference: I must seem very healthy. I guessed the odds to be about even; if my father brought it up with her they might go up. Two to one. My favor.

Friday afternoon she came to me in the living room, where I was in the wing chair and halfway through *The Fall of the House of Usher*. She had a red hot-water bottle in one hand and a bottle of citronella in the other. I had won!

In my room I got my knapsack down off the closet shelf. I had packed it the night before. I unbuckled it and took everything out so I could put the hot-water bottle in the bottom, then stuffed it again. She let me take the buffalo robe. I never did take that hot-water bottle out again till we returned home the next day. I don't think Peter saw it.

He asked to carry the buffalo robe when we went to the Royal to join up with King. I let him. He didn't think it was itchy at all.

The last thing King did was put a case of pop in the back of the McLaughlin, also two other bottles. As well there was a duck he'd dropped out of the morning rise at Yellow Grass slough.

"Wind shifted an' they all lifted off to the east—low, too, and in good range but the other end of the slough, an' the opposite direction. Just one goddam shoveller!" I could understand his disgust; spoonbills are bottom feeders going for sucker minnows and snails and frogs and blood-suckers and marsh grass; at their best they tasted just muddy and fishy. An Armenian child starving on cakes baked from mud and grass might think they were delicious.

Out of town a ways, King said, "Just heave it out into the ditch."

"Oh, no!" Peter said. He was on his knees and looking down on it in the back seat. "Can't we roast it, sir?"

"Suit yourself," King said. "You clean it."

"I will, sir!"

"Also—quit calling me 'sir'."

"Yes, sir."

"And slouch a bit more. One thing I can't stand or trust—it's a kid always says 'sir' and doesn't slouch."

"Righto!"

"That's better."

Just inside Muhlbiers', a short way from a caragana and poplar windbreak, King stopped the car. He leaned back and lifted the Boswell up out of the little jump-seat cradle there, and broke it open.

"You fellows circle wide and go to the far end of that windbreak. When I yell, the both of you start for me—just inside the edge."

"What for?" Peter was a fast learner.

"Prairie chicken." King shoved in two shells. "I'll squat down the other end. We'll see what you drive out."

Peter and I had just started into the windbreak when the

first prairie chicken went off, chittering and slapping, in a wide curve out from the caragana cover. We watched him plane down to a straw-stack a quarter-mile away. A minute later and further in we startled another that headed straight for the other end. We saw King rise up from squatting position, bring his shotgun to his shoulder. The prairie chicken veered away, then dropped as though he'd just discovered gravity. Then we heard the shot.

Halfway down, a whole covey exploded. King dropped two of them, one for each barrel.

"That's our supper, boys," he shouted.

We gutted and plucked them by the river bank, then took a swim. Peter came in after King and me, because he had to do his spoonbill.

"Couldn't we shoot a hare, too?" Peter said as we climbed into the McLaughlin. He meant a jack-rabbit.

"What for?"

"Our dinner."

"We got plenty," King said.

We had loaded firewood in the back, and after Peter and I had dropped off our sleeping-gear at the Mental hole we headed for the cave.

Bill came up as soon as King called him. Then Bill got down in the back as King told him to, and we drove back about halfway to the river.

"In case anybody sees our fire," King said. "Isn't likely— but if they do," he said to Bill, "you roll under the car. You fellows start building that fire. We're going to need a lot of coals."

We kept feeding the willow around the roasting-pan with the prairie chicken. King wouldn't let Peter put his spoonbill in with them, so Peter speared it with a stick and rested it across two forked ones and kept turning it. Half an hour before King figured the prairie chicken would be done, we buried potatoes in the coals. They came out pretty black, but with the prairie chicken they tasted lovely.

We heard a coyote. His untidy barking came first, then that long and lifting howl close as Brokenshell Grove maybe, though you could never tell for sure what direction it might be coming from, or how close or how far away he was, or whether he was just one or a couple or even three coyotes. Minutes later another answered him, much further away and to the south; he could have been sitting on the Montana border, and that was just fine with me.

King and Bill were on their third cup of coffee and Peter asked if we could have one too, but King said kids shouldn't drink coffee. That could be true about the coffee he and Bill were drinking, because they had something else in theirs besides canned milk and sugar. I didn't say that, because King didn't add that coffee could stunt my growth. I could still taste sage and maybe a touch of stinkweed from the prairie chicken. After all that prairie chicken, Peter and Bill had polished off the spoonbill between them, Peter chewing on it and smacking his lips and saying how smashing wild it tasted, though I noticed he had washed it down with a whole bottle of lime crush. When we bedded down later, I found out just how wild it had been, from the marshy ones Peter cut under the itchy buffalo robe.

'Willow smoke is the most lovely wood-smoke there is, I thought, especially mixed with King's Millbanks and the sweet smell of Bill's Old Stag tobacco juice, spattering the coals of our fire as regular as if he were Austin's grampa when he used to go down the street to get lost. The mosquitoes were bad, as my mother had predicted, even though we'd laid green leaves and branches over the fire for a smudge. It was difficult to get a position compromise right, between choking on smoke and being eaten up by mosquitoes. Peter and I and King were slapping them without a break. Not Bill. He simply sat and stared at the fire and spit and let the mosquitoes light and crawl all over his forehead and both cheeks, just drinking themselves full of his blood. Now and again he would grunt or he would bleat. That was all. It was as though he had made a sacred vow never to utter a word. I think I did hear him hum a couple of times that evening.

It was full night when King told us the story about the time a whole band of Indians were starving because the hunters couldn't find any game. A young chief, he said, left the band and went off by himself and built a saskatoon-sapling skeleton and covered it with hides. Inside, he fasted for three days and threw water on hot rocks till he went into a trance and a vision came to him. He went back to the others and told them that a herd of elk led by one great elk would appear, for he had seen them in his vision. He warned them that they must not shoot the lead elk.

The elk herd showed up at exactly the right time in exactly the right place and most of the hunters did exactly as the young chief said to do, except for one fellow who let fly at the great lead elk and dropped it with an arrow through its heart. In death it turned into the young chief.

"Red Indian legends are simply smashing!" Peter said.

"That's no legend," King said.

"Sure it is," I said.

"Nope."

"Having a magic vision and then turning yourself into a big elk—come on—then turning back into a human again!"

"Try it this way, Hughie. Game's scarce—hard to get— maybe a bad winter like the winter of 'six and 'seven, so most the game froze to death and what's left are real spooky. This fellow fasts and he sweats to clear his mind so he can solve the problem and he comes up with a great idea—way to hunt scarce game—a way nobody else ever thought of before."

"What way?"

"Decoy them! He got hold of a big rack of elk antlers and a elk hide—put them on himself so he could get close to them, then lead them right into ambush. Smart fellow. Only one out of that whole band smart enough to figure out what nobody else ever thought of before—*decoy* them—and that is just what he did, and it worked fine and that's why he warned them not to shoot the lead elk."

"Well, then, why did that son-of-a-bitch shoot him?"

"Greed maybe. Envy." King leaned forward and poked up the fire, then sat back again. "Fellow like that chief—he's dangerous too, you know."

Bill spit and it went *spurt-zzzzzip-aah*.

"If he can think up something the rest of them can't— makes him dangerous to the tribe."

"Why?" Peter said.

"Breaks their rules—takes a different direction from all the others. General run of chiefs, kings, heroes, they're shit-disturbers, so—once the war's won—dragon's dead— treasure's dug up—girl's rescued—danger's past—time to kill him off."

"Rotten of them."

"Way it is. Also—medicine can't last forever for one man.

They crucified Christ, remember—burned Joan of Arc at the stake—murdered Henry Hudson..."

There was a crack like a rifle shot and I felt a stinging jab in my right leg. Bill made a choking sound as though he'd swallowed his tobacco chew. His cup went flying, raining coffee. He jumped to his feet, his eyes wild in the moonlight and firelight, their whites turned right up, his back arched and rigid. He dropped. He opened and he closed like a jack-knife, with his legs kicking out and in again and again, and shoving the side of his head along the ground.

I smelled wool or hair singeing just as King grabbed him by the ankles and pulled him back from the fire edge. "Give me a hand!"

We did, and I guess with the practice we had washing Bill clean in the river, Peter and I were some help to King, who had Bill's head in his lap and was working at his mouth. I realized a minute later he was getting a hold of Bill's tongue and shoving a twig between his jaws so he wouldn't choke himself or bite his tongue off. I could feel the convulsions rippling through him as though he were a sheet on a line, then the fit wind died down and he buzzed like a gopher does after you get it a good one with a stick over the head. There wasn't any blood coming out of his nose, though.

"You going to give him a needle, King?" I said.

"Nothing to do with him being GPI—" King said. "He'll be all right now. You fellows better turn in—I'll stay with him."

"Can we have the flashlight?" I said.

"You won't need it—full moon." King was shining the flashlight on Bill, all over him, and you could see where the coals had scorched the back of his shirt before King had dragged him out of the fire. "Show you something." He moved his hand up from the back of Bill's neck, lifting the hair and training the flash on the bared scalp. "Shrapnel—surgery."

The scar tracked up past Bill's left ear, then over across the middle of his head. "He's got a silver plate in his head and that's why he takes his fits—my guess. Next time you fellows lay a fire, just make sure you clear out all the rocks first, so they don't go exploding hot coals and splinters in all directions."

"We did, sir," Peter said.

"Do it better next time. You could lose an eye that way."

"We will, sir," Peter said.

King had been right; we didn't have any trouble finding our way over the prairie and to the Mental hole where we'd left the robe and blankets and tarp. The whole river bank was winking green as though tonight was a firefly festival. Peter had never seen them before.

"Don't they have fireflies in England?"

"Not in High Wycombe they don't."

We picked them off the buck-brush and rose and wolf-willow leaves and held them pulsing in our palms.

"Let's capture a lot of them!"

"What for?"

"So we can put them into a little bottle and then use them under the buffalo robe for a torch!"

"You got a bottle?"

"No."

It was just as well, as I found out after Peter woke me up with a dandy spoonbill fart. No way I was going to put my head under that buffalo robe to see how well a firefly lantern might light up the dark. I had a hard time getting back to sleep, and the prairie chicken I'd eaten wasn't any help either; I couldn't light a single one to get even with him.

Before morning Peter woke me again, but this time it was because he had cramps. He never came back to bed really till daylight. It was the worst diarrhea he'd ever had, he said. It scalded. Which was all right with me.

X

By mid-August, almost a month since Bill had made his escape, most of the interest in him seemed to have died down. I don't think the Mounted Police were giving him any consistent attention; I think they'd stopped checking out empty granaries, barns, strawstacks. I know that the last time I'd heard my mother and father speak of him they had decided that he must have quit the district—or perished.

"Nobody's reported sighting him," my father said. "No break-ins for food. He's long gone—if he's still alive it will likely be in that badlands country between Tiger Lily and the border. That's where they'll uncover him—or his body. His mental condition, he couldn't possibly survive without institutional support."

That made me feel good, thinking that if it hadn't been for Peter and me and King, Bill would be lying dead in that butte country with the crows and magpies and coyotes feeding off him. Not only did I feel a little less guilty, but I also felt less apprehensive.

Austin Musgrave spoiled that, of course. Once he was through his quarantine I couldn't get unstuck from him. It made me almost anxious for the summer holidays to be over so that at least during school hours I wouldn't have to listen to him. There was no respite from him, because ever since we'd blown his grampa up in their backhouse, the Musgraves couldn't pry the old man out of his armchair by the front window of their living room. In the corner. There wasn't a chance of his going outside and wandering away and getting lost so that Musgrave would have to go looking for him so that I wouldn't have him on my back all the time.

"He'll never set foot outside the house again," Musgrave said. He'd stopped me halfway between their house and ours on my way to meet Peter to go out to the cave. "Doesn't say a word to anybody from morning till night. Just sits and stares out the window all day long." It seemed to me that Musgrave ought to be grateful that his grampa was cured of going outside to get lost. "All day long."

"I know that," I said. "Whenever I go past your house I can see him in there. . . ."

"All day long," Musgrave said again.

"Come on—he's got to go outside *sometime!*"

"No—he doesn't. . . ."

"Your house hasn't got inside . . ."

"I have to help him."

"Sometime he has to go outside to take a . . ."

"All the time now."

"Help him what?"

"Onto the bedpan."

"Oh." Now I could understand why Musgrave wasn't grateful.

"And off and empty it and the urinal too. Just too bad you and the other guys didn't listen to me when I said we shouldn't dig that cave in our back yard!"

Now just look who was lying. "You didn't say that!"

"Too bad Lobbidy supplied the boards. . . ."

"You were the one suggested it first! You said your grampa would still be having his afternoon nap, so if we all pitched in . . ."

"But Peter's the most responsible—he went and got those dynamite sticks. . . ."

"Look—you were the one *insisted* we had to use your yard after Lobbidy said he'd supply the boards, and again after the Liar said why didn't we dig it over at his place where the boards were so we wouldn't have to haul the boards from his place over to your place. . . ."

"You're all to blame."

There was an interesting thing I had discovered about Musgrave—not so much interesting, actually, as annoying; he was stubborn about imputing responsibility for everything. According to Musgrave, nothing simply occurred; a marble missed, a kite nose dived, rain fell on picnics, ice turned to rubber, fingers, toes, cheeks, or earlobes froze, races and

games were lost because of God. He not only *saw* little
sparrows fall; He dropped them. Yet, by Austinian reasoning,
God was Himself quite blameless. All fault must belong to
the sparrows who chose to peck oat seeds out of horse shit
and indulged in fluttering fornication in public. Musgrave was
skilled at aiming blame; he could draw and shoot it from the
hip. At somebody else.

According to Musgrave, God kept a meticulous ledger
up there. He liked good and bad things to balance out evenly.
Musgrave's favorite expression was: "We'll have to pay for it,"
or more often, "You'll have to pay for it." If you drowned out a
lot of gophers. If you had a beautifully kind Indian summer. If
you broke free of the dog-paddle. If you found a dime. You
would eventually have to pay for it. Not only would you have
to pay back ultimately with something bad happening to you;
it would be worse than the good thing was good. After
Christmas, Musgrave must have had to truly brace himself.
Given his usurious God, the odds were stacked against his
ever getting out of debt, even through public confession and
total immersion. At least the Catholics could make time
payments and had some hope of becoming morally solvent.

I always knew I was in for a tough time with Musgrave as
soon as he said who was to blame for something. He just kept
coming back at you.

"Didn't you."

"Didn't I what?"

"Spend all your time with Peter when I couldn't leave
the yard or have anybody come into it. Four times longer
than you and Peter. You guys didn't even get a week. What
did you guys do while I couldn't leave our yard all that time?"

"Went after gophers a few times—out to the Mental
hole. . . ."

"What else out there?"

"Just swimming."

"I saw you go by one Saturday."

"Yeah?"

"Afternoon."

"To the Hi-Art," I said.

"With a round-nose shovel?"

"Oh—that Saturday."

He waited.

"I was—that shovel—I was taking it back."

"Where?"

"Lobbidy's—I took his shovel by mistake instead of ours the day we blew up—we dug—did the first cave."

"You dug another one!"

"No."

"You said the *first* cave! You dug another one at Lobbidy's!"

"No we didn't!"

"Oh yes you did and left me right out of it while I was..."

"I just took back Lobbidy's round-nose shov—"

"Week after they turned him loose..."

"That's right...."

"... to go down to be with his Montana gramma! Did he need to take a shovel down to his..."

"His dad needed it!"

"What was the picture show?"

"William S. Hart. *The Cold Deck.*"

That stopped him. "I suppose you went to Chautauqua, you and Peter."

"Sure we did." I was still lying. "Every day." Peter and I didn't once go inside the great tent poking up in the empty lot next to Grace Methodist. It had been a deliberate and necessary sacrifice, staying away from the baked magic of canvas and the salad smell of crushed grass because we were too busy digging our cave, and finding Bill inside it, and running for King to help us, and then looking after Bill inside there. "What difference if we did, Musgrave? Other years your parents wouldn't let you go to Chautauqua—when you weren't quarantined, for blowing up your grampa in the backhouse!" Just as much as anybody, Peter and I would have enjoyed hearing the widow of the movie star Wallace Reid tell all about her husband's suffering and dying out of being a dope addict; the Liar had found it so exciting he didn't even claim Mr. and Mrs. Wallace Reid were his aunt and uncle. Also, I would have liked to hear the elocutionist tell about the boys who put the sneezing-powder into the preacher's handkerchief just before he recited "The Charge of the Light Brigade" so that the gallant six hundred, with cannon to right of them and cannon to left of them, sneezed all the way into the valley of death.

"They won't let me go to the Hi-Art either," Musgrave said quite sadly.

I knew that. He had already told me that the only time he had seen William S. Hart or Fatty Arbuckle or Charlie Chaplin was on the posters in front of the Hi-Art.

"Or Johnny J. Jones."

I also knew that, for he once told me that circuses were wicked; he had been unable to explain to me how clowns and camels and elephants and tigers could possibly be wicked. I don't think he really believed they were.

Now we were in front of my house because I'd turned us back, opposite the way I'd been going when he stopped me in front of their place. I was feeling quite sorry for him now, which might have explained why I told him the Presbyterian Sunday-school picnic had been rained out, so that we had to hold it in the church basement. That seemed to make him feel better.

"Just as well," he said.

"What do you mean—just as well!"

"Holy Rollers got their summer camp out at Brokenshell. It would be sacrilegious to have Presbyterian egg-and-spoon and three-legged and sack races when Holy Rollers were testifying and baptizing."

I didn't feel so sorry for him now. What he was really saying was that God rained out Presbyterian Sunday-school picnics but not Baptist ones. In fact He had rained out three Baptist Sunday-school picnics in a row, even though they were God's party too, since Baptist Sunday-school picnics were carefully adulterated with religious events like praying and hymn-singing. It was as though God had rained out His Face to spite His Nose.

I didn't say this to Musgrave. I said, "You want to play knife?" He wasn't very good at it, so I knew he wouldn't want to play it for very long.

"No. Let's go in your house."

"Hertha's afternoon off."

"So what?"

"My mother's out too."

"Playing bridge at Mrs. Marshall's." Musgrave really knew everything.

"At noon my mother said not to bring any kids into the house because she and Hertha had house-cleaned. . . ."

"And she's having them over to play bridge tonight."

"No. It's her evening for the Atheniums Annual and Perennial Flower, Book, Recipe, and Discussion Club."

"We won't mess it up."

"I promised."

"I got to use the toilet."

Because they had outdoor plumbing Musgrave was always interested in toilets. We had two actually: the one on the second floor with the bathtub and the little octagonal tiles on the floor and the walls, and the lone toilet bowl under the steps in the basement.

"Just do it between the lattice fence and the caragana."

"I got to do the other."

Perhaps. I took him in the side door and down into the basement. When he came out of the toilet he said as long as we were inside I might as well give him a ride in our dumb waiter, which ran up and down in a well between the basement kitchen and the breakfast room. Our meals were always interrupted by someone sticking his head inside the dumb waiter and shouting down to Hertha to send up the mashed potatoes or more gravy or the salt and pepper. It was hauled up and down by ropes in its sides, and went down a lot easier than it came up, especially with Austin crouched inside the box in the fetal position. After I had hauled him up and down about fifty times he said let's go upstairs. I said nothing doing. He said all right, but how about one last ride in our dumb waiter. I agreed. The box came down empty.

By the time I got up to the breakfast room, I heard him playing "Chopsticks." I went through the swing door into the dining room and then across the living room to the music room.

"Get off of that stool, Musgrave!"

He quit "Chopsticks." He started up "Dare To Be a Daniel."

"Get out of this music room and get out of our house!"

That stopped him. He turned round on the stool. "You don't like me, do you."

I almost answered him.

"You and Peter are good friends now and it happened while I was in quarantine." He made it sound as though it were wrong for me and Peter to be good friends. "And you've dug another cave and left me out of it."

I still didn't answer him.

"Didn't you?"

"Get out!"

He just looked at me. I looked right back. His eyes gave up first, sliding away from mine and up to Bach and Brahms and Liszt and Handel and Beethoven in their Circassian walnut frames. "I know. I'll find where."

"Bugger off!"

He buggered off. To make sure, I followed him to the front door and then watched him go down the street till he turned the corner. He knew, all right, and he'd really try to keep his threat of finding the cave. I had warned Peter that Musgrave would be our biggest problem, and I had been right. Now I wished we hadn't dug the cave; I wished we hadn't gone to King when we found Bill in there, and, oh, how I wished King hadn't suggested· hiding him. We were just kids, and King shouldn't have done that. It was really King's fault.

I had to get to Peter. I went back into the house through the front door, then out the side door. I checked that Musgrave hadn't circled round into our back yard before I went through the caragana to the alley.

Peter must have given up waiting for me. He wasn't at home. I didn't know what to do now. King had told us that if we ever had to go out to the cave and Bill without him, to be sure we went there together—never alone. We were to do that only when we thought it was absolutely necessary. Peter and I had decided it was necessary because we hadn't been out there for five days; for three of those days we hadn't been able to find King. We hadn't even seen his McLaughlin around town.

Bill couldn't be running out of food yet. King had really stocked him up the week before, and Peter and I had thrown down to him a couple of loaves of bread and some wieners and cheese a couple of days later. It wasn't that we worried he'd starve, but that if he got hungry he'd come out and start wandering and be seen. We already had him trained not to fill his water canteens at the river except after dark.

Perhaps Peter had gone out there without me.

He was nowhere around the cave. After I looked in the homesteader shack, I went over and bent down at the tunnel opening. The gamey smell of Bill came out quite strong to me. He was curled up down there and sleeping because I could hear him snoring. He was lucky; the day was a scorcher and it must be cool underground. Also, he was away from the mosquitoes and horse-flies, which were out in clouds.

Neither Peter nor anyone else was at the Mental hole. I headed upstream to the CPR bridge. Nobody there either. It must have been a hundred in the shade; my shirt and pants were sticking to me and my eyes were stinging with sweat. I undressed and dived in and stayed under; my whole body drank in coolness till my breath gave out. That gave me the idea of practicing it to the other side and back on one breath underwater. Because of this I almost got caught. I had just enough time to get out, grab up my clothes, and cover the open ground below the bridge to the shelter of the wolf-willow, rose, and buffalo-berry bushes.

Until then the worst thing I could think of happening to a person was to find himself in the center of an open field with Vonneguts' Holstein bull, magnificent, candy-pink knackers swinging, the savage and silly jewelry of the ring in his nose held low to the ground as he bore down on you in full charge. This was worse.

Sadie Rossdance and all the girls from her three little cottages had come down to the Little Souris. I counted seven of them as they walked right past me, not ten feet away. Including Sadie Rossdance. The rose and buffalo-berry bushes made a good, thick screen but their thorns had scratched and drawn blood; indeed one of the branches seemed to be pinned under me. Then I recognized the acid sting that was burning my stomach and the back of my right shoulder and my right arm to my elbow. By turning my head very carefully I saw the tall clump of hairy stalks and leaves: nettles. They weren't that close to me now, but when I had dived in they must have brushed across my shoulder and arm and stomach. Lucky I hadn't lain in them! Or got them in the crotch!

At first I thought the girls were going in wading, the way they sat down and began to unlace their shoes. As one they lifted a knee and reached up under their skirts and unsnapped garters, I guess. They rolled their stockings down and off. Almost together they stood, and then I realized they were not going wading. They crossed their arms; they stooped; they took the hem of their skirts; they straightened, lifting their arms as they did. They all stooped forward and pulled their dresses over their heads so that all stood in bloomers and brassieres and garter belts. They dropped their garter belts. They reached their arms down and then up behind themselves to undo their brassieres. In what followed I forgot all about the nettle stings.

It was as though breasts came in firecracker packages, and one braided fuse ignited by a punk stick set off a chain explosion of tits. I had not dreamed of their infinite variety: canteloupe, ice-cream cone, fried eggs, zeppelin. When they dropped their bloomers to their ankles, and stepped out of them, for the first time in my life I saw a naked female body. For the only time in my life I saw six of them at once. All the softness promised by upper arm and breast swell had been incredibly revealed to me in a profusion of straw-colored and unmistakably woman flesh.

I felt sick. Then—quickly—disappointed.

After all the years of wondering and wanting to see, there was nothing to see! Tits were quite unnecessary. They did not belong there. The whole female form was wrong! The shoulders were too narrow for the rest of the body, like Tweedledum and Tweedledee. Crotch hair hid everything. Unfortunately. Theirs was much tidier than a man's, ruled straight across the top on every single one of them. There were more black than blonde, and one of the first ones to walk out into the water carried an orange buzz between her thighs.

"All right now—Wanda—get on the other side an' you slip your arms under her! I'll put mine under the back of her head!"

The sick guilt feeling in me had stopped sloshing around.

"Just lay back—lay way back, Blanche! Stretch your arms out—keep your chin up! See! We're hardly holdin' you at all! You're ninety-nine an' nine-tenths floatin'!"

The perfume of wolf willow was all around me. Perfume sweet, yet musk wild! Many years later I would pin that lovely smell to a woman's sexual scent.

"Doin' great! I never saw anybody such a natural floater as you are, Blanche!"

Sadie Rossdance, still in her pink bloomers and brassiere, had her back to me. "Not too far out, Loretta! Closer to the bank—you'll go over your head there!"

"I can swim!"

"Dog-paddling isn't swimming!"

"See the moon rise! See the moon rise!" The girl who had gone out too deep to suit Miss Rossdance ducked and her white bum came up and over. She was the one that had the red crotch hair. She surfaced choking and sputtering, then coughing and holding her head desperately up and back.

"I told you! You're way out over your depth! Come on in shallower!"

Loretta stopped her frantic dog-paddling, and lowered her feet for the bottom that wasn't there. She sank out of sight, came up blowing, and did that quick eggbeater stroke till she was able to bottom it. She came out of the water toward Miss Rossdance. Her nipples were pink. They stood out like glass insulators on a telephone pole. I had a hard on.

"I warned you, Loretta—soon as I saw you dog-paddling. . . ."

"Breast stroke—goddamit!"

"Dog-paddle."

"Dog-paddle my ass!"

"I might at that," Miss Rossdance said. Her breasts sprang free as she loosed her brassiere strap. Flour sacks! She bent down and unrolled a towel at her feet. Then she balanced on one foot with the other held up. She was putting on rubber bathing-slippers. Both on, she stooped and this time came up with a bathing-cap. She pulled it on, then cocked her head first to one side and then to the other while she tucked up her hair underneath. The cap had a big red rubber peony over her right ear. Still wearing her bloomers she turned, but she did not walk towards the water. She was coming straight at me!

For a moment I thought of pulling back further into the bushes, then remembered the nettles. I hunched down tight and waited and prayed the half-praying you do that doesn't go beyond saying over and over to yourself, "Please, God—please, God!"

She kept on coming at me. I could see how the bathing-cap had lifted and puffed out her cheeks and pulled up on the corners of her eyes so that she looked almost Chinese. She stopped and she turned away and she squatted, sliding down her bloomers as she did. God must have heard me, because she kept facing out to the river bank. There came a slow and hissing sibilance and then that stopped, but she didn't stand up right away, not until she let go a fart. When she stood up she stepped out of her bloomers. The backs of her thighs and her buttocks were traced with blue veins, the flesh lumpy like badly made porridge.

As she walked away from my hiding-place, her great Roquefort buttocks alternating and asking for harness, I thought of the fire-wagon team and the town blacks Mr. Candy hitched to the honey wagon. I wondered if after she had finished her leak Miss Rossdance had opened and closed and opened and closed again like a camera shutter, the way mares did. Likely not.

I had lost my hard on.

She walked out into the river and stooped and scooped up water and splashed it on her upper arms and then on her front and lowered herself down to her chin. She did the breast-stroke with relaxed and deliberate dignity, holding the rubber red peony high out of the water.

"Vicky! You got a blood-sucker on you!"

"Where! Where! I can't see him!"

"Under your left . . ."

"Get him off me! Pull him off of me!"

"Poor little blood-sucker—suckin' off of Vicky."

"Pull him off!"

"He'll have a positive Wassermann now!"

They were playing tag and ducking each other and splashing each other except for one sitting near the edge and looking out to them. Two of the splashers in front of her were turned away from each other and making blind, backward swipes at the water. One of them missed the surface entirely to spin right round and lose her balance and go down. When she came up she said to the seated girl with the long, long black hair, "Come on in.

"Uh-uh."

"Can't you swim?"

"Sure." That's when I recognized her voice.

"Aw, come on in, Bella."

But Bella had her head down now and her arms out at her sides and her hands turned back at their wrists, sliding her palms back and forth as though she were smoothing out the water's surface.

The tag game had turned into a mud-throwing battle. They grabbed handfuls of it off the bottom and fired it at each other; most of the time they missed. One didn't, because

Bella stood up and took a charge right in the mouth. Loretta. Bella screamed, jumped into the water, and took out downstream after her. She caught up to her, grabbed her by the hair from behind and swung her round and round, then let her fly free to stagger a few steps and fall in the shallows.

"Give her hell, Loretta!"

"She asked for it, Bella!"

"Girls—girls! That's enough of that!" Nobody was paying any attention to Miss Rossdance at all; they had quit swimming or splashing to gather around Bella and Loretta facing each other where the river shallowed. Bella kept backing away until Loretta threw herself at her and she went over backwards with Loretta on top. Loretta stayed on top till Bella managed to roll Loretta over and hold *her* under. Then Bella let her up, coughing and spluttering and wiping at her face.

"Stop it! Stop it right now!" Miss Rossdance had them each by an arm, holding them apart.

"Aw, let them settle it!"

"I'm pullin' for Loretta!"

"There's nothing to settle! You girls make up!"

"She started it!" Bella said.

"I wasn't aimin' at you. . . ."

"Well—you *got* me!"

"You tried to drown me!"

"Right in the face!"

"Stop it—both of you!"

"Give it to her, Loretta!"

"Bust her jaw, Bella!"

"Don't back down from her, Loretta!"

"Now—Loretta—say you're sorry to Bell—"

"Kiss my Royal American!"

"And catch a dose off you!" Bella yelled.

"You never did clear up your first one!" Loretta hadn't seen Bella reach out behind herself and pull up a high cat-tail. She turned away as Bella swung it, but it caught her across the buttocks. Loretta pulled up a bulrush. All of them began to pull up bulrushes.

Sometimes out at the Mental hole what started out as reed-pipe fun turned mean and rotten: somebody might tease Blind Jesus and Buffalo Billy; almost every one of us had stuck a milkweed stalk up a frog's rectum and then inflated it, but it was not acceptable horror when Fat Isbister threw blown-up frogs onto the water to float till the sun tightened their belly skin and they exploded. We often had gang fights: wet shirt and towel fights, water fights, spear-grass fights, cow-pie fights. We had never even thought of cat-tail fights, the most spectacular of them all.

I watched the Sadie Rossdance girls pull up bulrushes with great, dripping divots of root and marsh muck. They pursued and ran from each other with water fanning out from their feet, frogs plopping ahead of them, and red-winged blackbirds frightened to flight. They flailed and they clubbed and they scimitared each other with wild and blind abandon, the brown and swollen bulrush heads bursting in clouds of drifting down that floated away on the wind. And as their fury grew, they forgot to change their grasp so that they could whip each other with the exploding cat-tail head; they simply pulled up and swung and scored with the slimy end, so that cheeks and foreheads and arms and breasts and thighs and buttocks and backs were smeared with mud slobber.

I saw Bella finally walk away from the cat-tail melee; at the marsh edge she stooped and pulled up a bulrush; she carried it swinging down by her side as she walked towards the railroad bridge, then up the embankment and out on the ties. She stopped. She stripped off the spear leaves. She broke off the roots. She clamped the four-foot length between her thighs.

"Hey Loretta!" Bella arched her back, which lifted the swollen cat-tail head higher. "Suck this one, Loretta!"

No one was fighting now, all of them looking up to Bella and laughing.

"Big one for you, Loretta!"

"Box like yours—you can easy handle that one, Loretta!"

They were all making fun of Loretta.

Bella jumped up and out from the railroad bridge and carried her long cat-tail erection all the way down to the water.

When her head broke clear of the water, even Loretta was laughing.

It took quite a while for them to clean themselves, bending and cupping up water to wash their faces and sluice down their fronts, turning around and getting each other to rub off where the sun had cooked it on their backs and buttocks, then diving under water to get it out of their hair.

From my hiding-place I watched them as they dried themselves off and towelled their hair, as they buttoned garter belts round their waists, then sat and rolled stockings up, then stood to step into bloomers and capture breasts and reach around and behind to fasten brassieres. They gathered up their towels and purses and headed in my direction.

"Why didn't Gert come?"

"Got the flag up."

That was Bella. She was not headed back towards town. It had been surprising to me that she had come swimming with them. It was astonishing that when they had finished she was not going back to the apartment in the Walker Block.

I thought that King would have been surprised too.

XI

It was about two weeks after King got the little bum lamb for Bill and Inspector Kydd shot his Russian wolfhound that my father came home for supper from the shop, and I knew instantly that something was wrong. I knew it from the way he did not answer me when he came in the front door and through the living room without even looking at me. It was not simply that he hadn't heard me say hello to him; there was an extra tightness about him that I could not read at all. It promised danger. To me.

As soon as we sat down I sensed that my mother knew something was wrong, even before Hertha had yelled up from below and my father went to the dumb waiter to haul our supper up. My mother did not ask my father if something had gone wrong again with the old press. There could be only one reason for that: the press was all right; I was not. My father's monosyllabic answers all through supper and his failure several times to answer my mother or me at all must have told her. What? Our cave, and Bill! I prayed that was not it. I was almost certain it was. I strengthened my efforts, short of conversation, to seem innocent and blameless.

From time to time I could feel both of them looking at me. I forced myself to look back at them and to smile. Neither of them smiled back at me.

"You're not hungry, son."

"Oh, yes!" That was much too enthusiastic, even without the apprehension that had made even the thought of food nauseating to me. I saw then that I had hardly touched my supper. I attacked it. I forked it in like a harvester, to prove I had told the truth about being hungry. When dessert came up on the dumb waiter and was set down before me, I dug right into that too, and several tablespoons too late I realized my mother was looking at me with disbelief.

For the first time I saw what the dessert was, and it was as though a dumb waiter inside me was about to bring it up a second time. "I don't mind it nearly so much now." I did. It was the most revolting food prepared since man's invention of fire: the gray-blue transparent stuff my father called "pickerel eyes"—tapioca.

He had not touched his. He shoved his plate ahead and got up. "When you're through, Hugh, I want to talk to you. In the den."

He came right to the point. "Tell me about the escaped Mental patient."

Briefly I thought of denying I knew a single thing about any escaped Mental patient. I just swallowed.

"Can you tell me anything about him?" he said.

"Not—very much." My father waited. "He's been escaped for a month—now."

"Yes?"

"They haven't caught him—yet."

"Why do you say—caught?"

"Uh—found—caught—yet." What was the great difference between being found and being caught?

"You any ideas why—he hasn't been?"

"No."

He waited. Deliberately. "What's bothering you, Hugh?"

"Nothing." When you are quite evidently bothered, it is not a good answer to say nothing is bothering you. "I broke another pair of glasses Wednesday."

He hadn't taken his cigar up from the brass ashtray; the long ash end of it was unflawed—like a tiny wasp's nest. "Better tell me, Hugh."

"I—Dad—I—don't . . . "

"Don't what?"

"Know—much—about him."

"What do you know?"

"Just—like about anybody else—I guess—he's escaped—they haven't been able to find him yet?"

"Have you any notion where he might be?"

"Same as anybody else—hiding—somewhere."

"Where?"

"Some barn maybe—empty one—not being used any more—granary—empty granary. . . ."

"There aren't any." I knew that, because there'd been two bumper crops in a row, and wheat and oats and barley had been going up and farmers were filling anything they could with grain. "Maybe he found one—anyway—that was empty."

"It is difficult to understand how an insane man has been able to elude the police for over a month—without someone helping him. Where is he getting his food? How is he getting it?"

"Maybe he's gone—isn't in our district any more."

"That's possible."

"Or—maybe he's dead. Somewhere."

"Also possible. But they haven't found his body, and that doesn't make any sense."

"Maybe he drowned in the river."

"You know they dragged the river—three weeks ago."

"Oh—yeah."

"Chief Van Wart dropped into the shop this afternoon. He has a theory. Something Irma said to him . . ."

"Irma stinks!"

"She told her father some boys were doing something out on the prairie some time ago—she also overheard some boys talking about the patient . . ."

"That's all anybody talks about most of the time!"

"Chief Van Wart said that Irma told him—that you were one of the boys."

"She didn't see . . ." I stopped just before I would say she hadn't seen Peter and me and Bill under the CPR bridge at the South Saskatchewan Holy Roller baptizing in the Little Souris. ". . . Peter and me naked swimming in the river at the CPR hole!"

"Were you one of the boys Irma was telling her father about?"

"I guess. I could of been. She's always talking about me. She says my soul is dirty."

My father picked his cigar up and knocked the long ash off into the tray. That was a good sign. "Chief Van Wart wanted to know what I thought of a possibility he'd thought of."

Even though I didn't really want to know what Chief Van Wart thought, I said, "What possibility?"

"Some boys might have been helping to hide..."

I let the tapioca go, most of it, into the waste-basket. It had not been necessary to help it very much.

After my father had let go of my forehead and given me his handkerchief, he said, "I hate the goddam stuff too." That was a second good sign.

"Don't get me wrong, Hugh. I simply thought you might have heard something—that you might know something you hadn't told us." That was a hell of a lot different the way he'd been talking before I vomited the tapioca.

He said he guessed it would have to be older boys than me and Peter, and that it was probably an outside possibility anyway. Also, the old press had broken down that afternoon.

XII

After the shock of discovery I recalled that I had felt apprehension even before I got out to the cave. Since anxiety and fear were my most usual emotions that summer, it was quite likely I had expected trouble even before I had left town and started over the prairie. My stomach always knotted up whenever Peter and I made our visits out there. I was not ready, however, for horror.

My first thought was: "Why did it have to be me! Alone!" My next was: "I want my dad!"

I had called first at Peter's, and the yellow quarantine sign Chief Holroyd had nailed up on the Deane-Cooper front door was the first I knew that Peter had come down with chicken-pox. The scarlet-fever sign was always red. Peter's mother said I must not come inside to see him, and I said it was all right because I'd already had my chicken-pox the summer before, and she said it wasn't that I might catch it from him but that Peter was running a very high temperature and Dr. Sinclair had said that he must not be disturbed.

Out on the sidewalk I looked back up and saw that the blinds on Peter's bedroom were pulled. When I had chicken-pox my mother had done that for me, too, so no light would strike my eyeballs and blind me for the rest of my life. As I walked down Sixth I counted three more placards, one of them on a Musgrave porch post. I was a little ashamed of myself that I felt suddenly relieved, if not glad, knowing I wouldn't have to worry for a couple of weeks about Musgrave finding our cave with Bill in it.

If someone caught a disease, through no fault of his own, why did the whole world have to be notified? It made me think of the olden days in the Bible when God went around spilling boils and leprosy on people to get even with them. I don't mean He used scarlet fever, chicken-pox, mumps, measles, infantile paralysis, pink eye, and diphtheria instead of leprosy today, but the quarantine poster accomplished nearly the same thing as tinkling a little bell and crying, "Unclean! Unclean!" After Musgrave first told me about venereal diseases, I remember thinking how considerate they were not to nail up announcing placards for clap on the front of people's homes.

As I walked alone past the Fairgrounds and the Mental Hospital, I don't think my feeling of apprehension was any greater than it had usually been that summer, whenever I went out to our cave, and Bill, with Peter and King. I anticipated trouble always, disaster often, true horror not quite yet. Until that afternoon.

Without suspecting it, I smelled it from possibly a quarter of a mile away; if the wind had been to me and not a cross one, the shit incense of death would have reached me sooner. Even then I would not have taken it seriously, for the first discovery of mortality is given early to a prairie child. We were by the age of twelve quite used to that smell—or rather, smells; they could vary so in revulsion weight, depending on time and distance and creature size: gopher, cat, dog, jackrabbit, badger, skunk, coyote, horse or cow, near or far, putrid rot smell of new, to slightly soured straw smell of old, death, long after crows and magpies, beetles and maggots, and other prairie undertakers were through their work. By ten we could tell what had been at a larger cadaver, whether crow or magpie, bobcat or coyote, for the coyote always began to eat out at the anus, the bobcat at the soft belly, magpies almost anywhere. The Liar said they always went for the eyes first.

I walked to within a hundred yards of the cave and there I stopped when I caught a signal of white, as though someone had dropped a handkerchief low in the wild-rose bush with its orange haws like Christmas-tree lights. Then I saw that our straw and chicken-wire lid had been dragged off the tunnel mouth. Using all the willpower I owned, I forced myself closer. Then I stopped. Then I stopped being a boy.

The white was bone, a leg with only part of the foot left and the flesh gnawed off from the ankle to the knee! He must have had one of his fits and died down in there and the coyotes had smelled him, had entered and dragged backwards on him, by one foot, hind legs and dog rump working, till the rest of Bill's body jammed in the tunnel.

Gophers clubbed till their milk eyes marbled out, cats showing needle teeth in a final grin, lump-jaw steers bloated rotten or mummified to hair and skin and bone by the prairie kiln of wind and sun, had not prepared me for this inevitable vision given to me too young. The same terrible revelation must have been given King at sixteen in France: the ultimate corruption of human death.

I ran all the way to town, then to the print shop and my father. He shut down the press turning out invoice forms and took me with him to Inspector Kydd in the RCMP barracks. Barney Elderfield drove us to get our car at our house, then followed us out Government Road to Muhlbiers' and over the prairie, behind us other cars, Mr. Nightingale with basket and hearse, the town dray with men and shovels, boys on bicycles and boys on foot; "Word of death and gold travels quickly," my father said later.

On the way out I told him everything.

The town sewer-diggers dug our tunnel out.

Alive with maggots, black with clotted blood, bruised like an apple and keg-swollen, the head was no longer a head, flies wandering in and out of what had once been eyes, nostrils, mouth, ears; this body was not Bill's.

It was Bella's.

There were several sessions with my father in his den. He asked me why we had done it and I said we had sort of slid into it. He asked me why we had sort of slid into it, and I said I didn't know why we had. He asked me whose dumb idea it was to begin with, and at first I said it probably belonged to both Peter and me, but I ended up admitting that it had been King who suggested we keep Bill in our cave, and that Peter and I had gone along with it. He asked me why we had gone along with it, and I said I didn't know why we had but we had. And now, he said, just look at the consequences. I started to cry and said I had seen Bella's head and what the coyotes had done to her leg, and he put his arm around me and pulled me to him.

The next time he asked me why again, and I said I didn't know why, and then I said it was because we had just wanted to help Bill and that was all, and he said didn't I think we would have helped him more if we had reported our discovery right away, so that he could have been returned to the Mental for care. I said yes, I guessed, it would have been better if we had done that, and he asked again why we hadn't done it, and I said I didn't know why we hadn't done it, and he said if we had done it perhaps Bella would still be alive and they wouldn't be trying to find Bill so they could keep him from killing somebody else. I cried again.

My father came with me when I had to go to the barracks so that Inspector Kydd could question me. Peter was still quarantined for his chicken-pox. I had never been inside the RCMP barracks before, and was surprised that it was nothing unusual, just an office with a long counter and Constable Barney Elderfield behind it. I knew they had a cage in the basement. My father and I went through the low swing-gate at one end of the counter and Barney took us into Inspector Kydd's office, which, like my father's den, smelled quite strongly of pipe smoke. It also smelled like Riddle's Shoe and Harness. Also like a kennel. A Russian wolfhound was curled up on the floor to one side of Inspector Kydd's desk.

Actually it was easier being questioned by Inspector Kydd than it had been by my father. He didn't seem to want to know *why* we had hidden Bill, just details about hiding him. He asked his questions over and over again, too. Barney Elderfield had a notebook and he wrote down everything that was said.

My father asked if there were going to be any charges laid against me and Peter.

"I really can't say."

"I would like you to say," my father said.

"I'll know better after the inquest."

Will the boys be needed for the inquest?"

"Yes."

"After the inquest," my father said, "do you think there will be any charges laid against the boys?"

"After the inquest..."

"... you will have just about as much information about the boys' part in this as you have right now."

Inspector Kydd stared across his desk at my father for a moment, then he stood up. Barney Elderfield closed up his notebook and he got up.

"You haven't answered my question, Inspector."

"No, I haven't." Inspector Kydd started round the end of his desk. He had to step over the dog.

"They are a stupid breed, aren't they," my father said.

"Yes," Inspector Kydd said. He put his hand on my father's arm. "I don't think it's likely."

I heard my father's breath release in a sigh.

They held the inquest in Mr. Mackey's room in Haig School and Dr. Sinclair sat at Mr. Mackey's desk. They didn't make anybody swear on the Bible. Peter was over his chicken-pox, so he was invited inside with me. This was the fourth time I had been asked the same questions, only it was Dr. Sinclair this time. We didn't get a chance to see or hear the rest of the inquest, which decided that Bella had died as a result of being bludgeoned to death with a blunt instrument, probably at the hands of an escaped mental patient. Bill.

Before or after the inquest, not once did my mother talk with me about it; I think it must have been the only time she ever left everything entirely up to my father, and I think that must have been her own decision. It was my father who told me that I was not to go near the Royal Pool Hall till I was seventeen. He also said that I would probably not be playing hockey that winter, since he did not care to have me coached by King Motherwell. As well, I was not to go out of my way to associate with Peter any more than necessary, on or off the school grounds.

XIII

Sir Walter Raleigh threw the Boys' and Girls' doors open and our summer holidays were over. Mr. Mackey lined us all up in the hallway and gave the ant-and-grasshopper and obligation-ladder speech. I had been promoted out of Miss Coldtart and into his room, and not until that fall had I heard his "The Old Steeplejack and the Young Steeplejack" speech. I'd heard *about* it from the older boys, but this was the first time I heard him give it, since he saved it only for members of his own class. It seemed he had once known two steeplejacks, one named Charlie, one named Norman. Charlie was an old and experienced steeplejack, but Norman was a young and inexperienced steeplejack apprenticed to Charlie. They started out to climb a very high church steeple with Charlie, the wise old steeplejack, going up hand over hand, and Norman, the dumb young steeplejack, bringing up below. On and on and ever upwards they climbed, getting higher and higher up that very tall church steeple they intended to paint. Three-quarters of the way up there, Norman made a stupid mistake. He looked down. Instantly he became dizzy with vertigo; the whole world far below him spun round and round, and just as he was about to lose his grasp and plunge to his horrible death below, he heard a deep and reassuring voice come down to him from above, "Don't look down, Norman. Look up.

Mr. Mackey stopped for quite a long while, then he said, "What lesson may we learn from Charlie, the wise old steeplejack, and Norman, the young and inexperienced steeplejack?"

Irma Van Wart's arm shot straight up and the right side

of her fat ass lifted six inches off her seat, and Mr. Mackey didn't see it. Her hand. He said that he expected every one of us to look upwards in whatever we did. In school or out of school. For the rest of our lives. Which is one hell of a good way to get creamed on the ice at the Arena, Lobbidy said afterwards.

Mr. Mackey turned us loose early with our supply list for the school year. We trooped down to McConkey's Drugs to be issued scribblers, pencils, erasers, and pen-nibs, our new readers and paintboxes and geometry sets. This year's copybook for Writing had changed the way you must make your capital letters. Again. We came back after the noon break to sloping desk-tops that still held cake and cookie and bread crumbs, and the whole classroom smelled of pickles, apples, beef, and strawberry jam, from the farm kids' lunches.

Down in Montana, Lobbidy's gramma had given him a horse. The Liar said his great-uncle on his mother's side had dug the Panama Canal, so that was one of his relatives that had been pretty busy during the summer; I guess it must have been from that side of the family that his sister, Vera, had got her very big brain.

Our first composition class Mr. Mackey gave us the topics we could use for our first essay.

I knew how Norman must have felt when he looked down from his church steeple, when I looked at the first topic he wrote on the board: HOW I SPENT MY SUMMER HOLIDAYS. Lobbidy picked MY FAVORITE PET, but I couldn't use that one, because my mother wouldn't let me have a guinea pig, let alone a cat or a dog or a horse. I had to settle for I WAS A CANADIAN TEN-CENT PIECE, which the girls always picked, though it did occur to me that if I were a Canadian ten-cent piece I might have been given to Irma Van Wart and she would have tied me in the corner of her handkerchief and I would have smelled like fire-horse shit till I got handed on to somebody else.

With September here, each dawn and dusk had become hysterical as the prairie sky unravelled along its north horizon edge, in line after wavering line of wild geese flying and crying south.

I got strapped in Mr. Mackey's office for sliding down the tin fire-escape.

Now that harvest war had been declared all over the

prairie, burning straw-stacks sent up their Indian signals by day, and glowed like giant Drake beacons by night. Neither man nor child nor bird nor beast defied the seasons here.

Peter got the strap three times before the end of September. The first Monday-morning recess he came over to me by the little kids' swings and teeter-totters, and I felt a lovely lift inside me, that he ached to talk with me as much as I wanted to talk with him. Probably his father and mother had warned him to stay away from me.

"Did you *have* to tell your father everything?"

All the time I had known him, he had never looked at me like that before.

"Been much simpler if you hadn't, you know." His voice didn't even sound angry. It was as though he were saying, "By the way, your fly's unbuttoned," and he couldn't care less.

"After I found her—I had to tell him!"

"Not really. Just report the body then shut up."

"You would have told—too!"

"I stand by my chums. You should have too. Shouldn't have been all that difficult to let them think it was Bill's own cave—that he dug it to hide in it—after he escaped. . . ."

"For six weeks! Getting his own food and water!"

"Let them worry about that. They'd have assumed it was his cave if you hadn't told."

"And you wouldn't!"

"I would not."

"You just *think* you wouldn't! But you would of! If it was you found her—don't go telling me that's all you would report—that you found a dead body in a cave!"

"Yes."

"Easy for you to say that when it wasn't you found her! You don't know what you're talking about!"

"All the same . . ."

"Oh—I only wish it had of been you! And if it was, Deane-Cooper, I'll tell you something—you'd do just what I did, and afterwards I wouldn't say to you what you just said to me! Afterwards you wouldn't hear that kind of bullshit out of me!"

Even before recess was over, I knew that he probably would have done just what he said he would. I also realized that in all the time I'd known him, that was the first time I'd called him Deane-Cooper instead of Peter.

I guess it hadn't been easy for him, either, knowing that whenever his back was turned, people were talking about what he'd done that summer. No one ever came right out and asked about it; indeed it was as though Peter and I had been told by the doctor that we hadn't very long left to live, and everybody did his best not to remind us of it. Except for Musgrave. It was also as though people thought they might catch something off of us. I suppose King must have been getting the same sort of treatment. I wouldn't know for sure, because I wasn't supposed to see him any more.

The search was on for Bill again, only much harder than it had been before he'd beaten Bella to death. Inspector Kydd called in extra Mounties from Moose Jaw and from Swift Current to help him and Barney Elderfield. Almost daily you'd see them riding out of town and onto the prairie around. They didn't take the Russian wolfhounds out with them, but only, I suppose, because the breed was specialized for quarry like coyotes—not humans.

They did not drag the river the way they had done when Bill made his escape from the Mental, but they staked out his place in the badlands. They took out a half-page notice in *The Gleaner* three weeks running, saying Bill was dangerous and could be armed, and warning all farm people to lock up carefully, and asking everyone to report anything unusual that might be helpful, and to phone this number. The same notice was tacked up in the CPR depot, and Bill had joined the WANTED posters in the Post Office. He was wearing a soldier hat.

"They're sure to get him," Musgrave said. "The Mounties always do. Unless somebody's hiding him again."

Another time Musgrave said to me, "They'll never capture him alive, but it doesn't really matter. If they don't get him before winter comes, he'll freeze to death out there. Serve him right."

Thinking of Bella's head and the black band grieving on King's left arm, I suppose it would.

My mother had never talked with me about it; she simply looked at me a great deal more often than usual. As far as she was concerned, I think she had made up her mind very early that her innocent son had been drawn, probably against his will and conscience, into the dreadful thing initiated by King Motherwell and Peter Deane-Cooper. In a very short time she would move on from "that's what might have happened" to "that's how it must have happened" to "that's what happened" to "the whole thing didn't happen at all." That fall I wished I had inherited that blessed ability at self-deception from her.

I was in trouble. I was in it way over my age depth. During the day was bad enough, but night-time was worse. As long as I could remember I had been afraid of the dark, and hardly needed finding Bella in our cave to give me nightmares. Hi-Art serials and *Chums* had already done that for me. For several years my mother and I had been engaged in a continuing contest in which she tried to win me to sleep before nine o'clock on school-next-day nights and ten on Fridays and Saturdays. My main weapon was a flashlight which I could take under the covers, there to read about English boys, who stained themselves with walnut juice, put on sheets and turbans to sneak disguised into the dangerous native quarter to be captured by thugs, who lowered them into pits simply crawling with stinging scorpions or deadly hooded cobras. A hundred years ago in black tricorn hats and hair queues and blouses that had full sleeves caught at their wrists, with flashing swords and blazing pistols they duelled bearded and eye-patched pirates who marooned them or set them adrift in open rowboats to be embraced by great, suckered octopus arms. Rowboat included.

Opening my eyes to the dark in my bedroom got rid of the octopus, but it could not save me from the horror of Bella's head, of that white leg-bone and her half-eaten foot in the tunnel mouth of our cave. Several times that fall I woke up yelling, and my mother came in to me and held me in her arms till I'd stopped shaking. She would wipe the sweat off me with a towel and ask me again if I wanted to come into bed with her and my father, and I would have to say no. I knew I was too old for that.

In time the nightmares came to me further and further apart, but my fear of the dark did not diminish. If I made the grave mistake of failing to go to the bathroom before I went to sleep and later woke up, only the pressure of urine urgent enough to drive a stylite down could get me to lower my feet to the cold floor, where I knew a robber or a crazed murderer lay waiting to reach out from under the bed and grab me by the bare ankle. I could no longer trick my fear by telling myself that wicked people robbed and wounded and killed only adults and never children.

I now realize they often do and that Saint Simeon just had to piss off his pillar and out into the dark.

I had a clever idea. After the nightmares had stopped, if I woke in the middle of the night and had to go to the toilet, I screamed as *though* I were having a bad dream. Besides frightening any crazy murderer away, it always brought my mother on the run, and she would turn on the light. I must have overdone it because late in November it was my father came to me.

"All right, Hugh, just quit it!"

The next night I had a real dandy one. Neither of them came in to me, but I lived through it.

At breakfast the next morning my mother said she was very worried about me and that a growing boy needed every bit of sleep he could get, and that she had a good idea.

"What idea?"

"If you had someone in there with you—at night."

"Yeah—that would be great!" Then I had an idea. "Not you!"

"Of course not!"

"Dad!" I wouldn't have minded that.

"No."

Hell! She meant Hertha!

"You're an only boy," my mother was saying; "if you had brothers—a brother—you could share a bedroom with him. Maybe—if we could—it might be wise if we found someone to come over and spend the night with you, and—perhaps— sometimes you could go over to his place."

"Sure!"

"Want to give it a try?"

That would be great, having Peter to stay overnight with me and going to his place to stay with him!

"Austin Musgrave's mother . . ."

"What!"

" . . . she says she's willing for . . ."

"Not Musgrave! . . ."

" . . . Austin to come over here with . . ."

"Peter!"

"Austin!"

"No—Peter!"

"It is all arranged! Austin!"

I could not unglue her resistance. She had no intention, she said, of letting Peter come over so we could both enjoy our nightmares together. As a matter of fact, she said, she was forbidding me even to play with Peter again. My father had already told me that. I quit while I was still losing. Right after school that same day, Musgrave arrived at our house with his toothbrush and a pack of Old Maid cards. He was allowed to play cards so long as it was with a Snap or Old Maid deck that didn't have kings and queens and jacks and jokers for face cards.

He got me to pull him up and down between the breakfast room and the kitchen, crouched with his knees under his chin in our dumb waiter. Five times. He got me to go up to the billiard room so he could see the settee and two chairs for which a herd of elk had died. He got me to take off my boots so we could climb up on the table and fire the ivory balls down the felt at each other's toes to score. He won. He got me to play Old Maid with him, and in the middle of the third game he told me that my mother and all the ladies in her bridge club would probably end up in hell.

I said it would have to be a pretty fancy hell with ladyfingers, brownies, mocha cakes, and cucumber, olive, and walnut sandwiches with their crusts cut off, and I wasn't interested in playing Old Maid with him any more.

He asked me what did Bella look like when I found her in the cave Peter and I dug, and I told him to shut up about that.

He did. Then he started up on venereal disease, which was preferable to Bella or my mother and all her bridge-playing friends headed for hell, with their Royal Crown Derby teacups and saucers.

"Mainly one way to catch it," he said.

Even though I knew, I said, "How?"

"Fornication."

"What's that?"

"With a girl. They do it in the Bible."

"Who?"

"Fornicators—harlots."

"What's a harlot?" I already knew that one too.

"Female fornicator."

"You mean out of screwing."

"Yeah."

"Piece of tail."

"Yeah."

"Piece of ass."

"Yeah."

"Fucking." That was what I had been waiting to spear him with.

He didn't answer that one. My mother called us down to supper.

After supper, he asked me again in the living room what Bella looked like. I said just shut up about that. He did, but I knew he'd ask me again. Musgrave reminded me of a toy drum I got one Christmas, with clown faces painted on each end of it. When you sat or kneeled on the floor and shoved it hard away from you, it got slower and slower as the push energy died down, hesitated, then with increasing speed rolled right back to you. Just like that, again and again Musgrave came back at you.

He asked about Bella again just before we went to bed.

"I'm going to punch you right in the face, Musgrave— you ask me again." He had to take me seriously. There wasn't much room for him to run in our bathroom. He bent over the basin and started brushing his teeth. For fifteen minutes. From all angles, while I waited for my turn.

He finally squirted out toothpaste and spit. "Ssspurutt— said the goose."

I just happened to know that goose shit was green—not white.

It was no use getting up off the toilet lid. He was gargling. Then he was soaping the washcloth and doing his face and his neck. Then he made thick lather and drew the washcloth into a point and loaded lather on the end of it and speared it up each of his nostrils and swabbed it round in there. Then he cupped water in both hands under the tap and lifted it and snuffed it up. Then he put a thumb on each side of his nose and blew the result out. Then he did each ear. Then he turned away from our basin.

I started brushing my teeth.

"Did she have her bloomers on?"

I blew toothpaste at him, but I missed.

"I'm your guest!" he said.

"Not after tonight!" I said.

"You don't like me, do you!"

"That's right!"

"You and Peter didn't let me in on your cave!"

I walked out of the bathroom. He slammed the door behind me.

It was a good twenty minutes before he came to bed. It was all right with me if he needed that much private time to soap out his ass-hole and do his foreskin too.

"I'm sorry I asked you, Hughie." He had climbed into bed beside me. "I won't ask you again. It must of been awful seeing a dead person like that, and I'm glad your mother asked my mother to let me come over with you so you wouldn't have any more nightmares. I'd want you to sleep over with me if it had been me. You're the first person I'd want. Way ahead of Lobbidy or Angus or the Liar. And you're the first one I always think of inviting if I have a birthday party. I always liked you, Hughie."

"Go to sleep."

"Sure."

He had not said his prayers.

He did not mention Bella again, and even though it was Musgrave, I knew that having him in bed with me, I wouldn't likely be afraid of the dark that night.

"If my mother lets you, will you come over and stay with me at our house?"

"Maybe."

"Can I come over here again?"

"I guess so."

"Good night, Hughie."

"Good night."

He had still not said his prayers.

We didn't go to sleep right away, because my bed was a brass one and we put pillows on the rails for saddles and pretended we were William S. Hart and Indians and fell off our horses when the other guy shot us. It was a little childish but it was fun. I let Musgrave have the high one at the head of the bed. My mother came in and told us to settle down now. Three times. Then we did.

He had not yet said his prayers.

It wasn't easy to keep from falling asleep before Musgrave did. When I figured he had, I said, "Musgrave."

He didn't answer me.

"Austin."

"Mmmh."

"You forgot." I was having a hard time deciding whether to tell him now or not to tell him until in the morning. I waited while I made up my mind. "Austin."

He didn't answer me. I reached my hand over and I shook his shoulder.

"Austin."

"I know."

"Huh?"

"I didn't forget."

"You did so!"

"No. Isn't time yet."

"Huh?"

"I always wait."

"What for?"

"Till I almost fall asleep."

"Why?"

"I'm training my will-power so I can even go to sleep and then sleep a few seconds and then make myself wake up and then make myself get out of bed and kneel down and say them."

"Oh." I didn't want to believe him, but I knew he was telling the truth. "Why?"

"That way I figure it God is more likely to notice me. If I'm the only kid in the whole world that does it, then He's likely to notice I'm the only one that does it. If He's worried about me not saying my prayers, then He'll pay me special attention. Appreciate me."

"Why should He?"

"Because He goes in for sacrifices. I also burn my toast sometimes."

"What!"

"Deliberately. That's my *burnt* sacrifice to Him. One time I let my oatmeal scorch—on purpose."

I believed him. I was feeling a little sorry for him now. It did not last long.

"Now I am wide awake and it's your fault. If you minded your own business, then I would have just waited and then forced myself to get up and kneel down in the dark on the cold floor to say 'Now I Lay Me Down'."

"*Frozen* sacrifice."

"Yeah. You need it a lot worse than me."

For quite a while I kept myself awake to see if Musgrave really did get to sleep, then force himself awake, then climb down out of bed in the dark to say his prayers, but I fell asleep. Son of a bitch probably did. I didn't remember till next morning that I hadn't said my own bedtime prayers that night.

Before the end of the week I told my mother I was fine now and didn't need anyone to sleep over with me. I realized there were worse things than being afraid of the dark. Having Musgrave sleep over with me was one of them.

After four one Thursday early in October, I made up my mind there was something I had to do. By myself. I didn't really want to, but I felt I ought to go out to where we'd hidden Bill and I had found Bella. I willed myself down Sixth.

At McNernys' corner I caught the sour ferment of fallen leaves from their caragana, then stepped out into the road because Daisy Inwards and Aileen McNerny and Ruby Wilson were crouching in the middle of the sidewalk and bouncing their balls and scooping up jacks. I kept walking down the middle of the road till I had to get over for Inspector Kydd and Mrs. Inspector Kydd and the two wolfhounds behind them. Mrs. Inspector Kydd's horse had its tail up, and just as he passed me his ass-hole opened slowly like a black rose blooming. He dropped a slow string of four, and I was thinking how cleanly a horse did it compared to other animals, like a cow, for instance, that just lets it slather down her leg as though she didn't give a shit how she shit. Also, horse manure didn't smell all that bad. Even fresh. Perhaps sheep's was even better than horses'. Humans' had to be the worst smell of all. And Bella!

I wished that something would happen that would give me an excuse not to keep on going out there! Maybe Lobbidy would come down Government Road, leathering both sides, and invite me to climb up. During his summer holidays he'd got a gelding for his birthday, and the two weeks left to swim he had let me ride up behind him when we went out to the Mental hole. He didn't do much swimming or diving out there, just sat on his horse in the Little Souris, up front and

aked like a mahout on an elephant in the Ganges. Lobbidy
aid it was what they called a Montana pony, but it looked
ust like a buckskin to me. It had lovely hooves like black
eacups. He said he was hoping for a saddle at Christmas.

Musgrave said buckskins were generally mean and that
Lobbidy likely would end up bow-legged the rest of his life,
and I said I wouldn't mind being bow-legged if I could have a
horse and if Musgrave's parents gave him one he could maybe
not turn out bow-legged, and Musgrave said how—and I said
or him to just ride it side-saddle, like Mrs. Inspector Kydd
did.

When I left him at his house, he got me a good one in
he back of the head. I never could make up my mind
whether it was worse to get hit with a Musgrave road-apple in
he winter when they really hurt, or in the summer when
hey got in your hair. One thing I was certain of: Musgrave
could throw and he could run.

At the Catholic-church corner I turned towards down-
own instead of the Fairgrounds. Perhaps I ought to go in the
print shop and see how my father was doing before I went out
o our cave.

"Shut the door behind you, Hugh. Can get drafty in
here." He was at the hand press. "Persephone's getting ready
o go downstairs."

"Who's Persephone?"

"Demeter's daughter."

"Who's she?"

"Ceres in your *Golden Book of Legend*. The manic-
depressive goddess, who gave you oatmeal porridge and
winter so you can curl and play hockey."

"You won't let me play..."

"That's right. Sorrowing for her daughter, so she's ready
o wander again. You want to stack those 'No Hunting' and
No Trespassing' signs on the shelf for me?"

I did. I also swept out the shop for him without being
asked to; because it was Thursday he wouldn't get *The
Gleaner* or himself to bed before midnight.

I went into Chan Kai's and got a fried-egg candy and a
icorice whip and cigar with those little red seeds on the end
so that it looks like it's burning. Eating them almost took my
mind off what I had to do. Until Cavanaugh's Livery Stable. I
stood there for quite a while.

On great iron wheels a tractor rolled past me down Government Road, breathing steam like the head of a straw-eating dragon. Behind it came the great threshing machine, followed by a long and rattling tail of linked bunk-house, cook car, and empty bundle-racks. God, how I wished I wasn't afraid of the dark, and wished I had the guts to go out to the cave! King would sure be ashamed of me if he knew!

Half the animal trainer's tiger was gone, pasted up on the face of Cavanaugh's Livery barn two summers before, when Johnny J. Jones had come and gone from our town. Even the fall before, I remembered, one lower corner had come loose and torn off in the wind; the ringmaster in his tail coat and white kid pants and top hat had faded by then. So had the tamer with his looped whip and kitchen chair and the tiger on his upturned pail, jaws open and lips curled away from the great incisors, head archly tilted, one great paw ready to swat.

Maybe Johnny J. Jones would come back to us next summer, but that was a long way away, and Peter thought I was a cad for telling, and Bill had beaten Bella to death, and I would never be friends with King again, and I was crying in front of Cavanaugh's Livery barn.

Poor little son-of-a-bitch Hughie in horn-rimmed glasses for his lazy left eye. Forlorn—forlorn—forlorn! Like an old circus poster all forlorn!

First frost had got the necks of the sunflowers along the edge of the Fairgounds racetrack, and their clock heads hung. On the prairie beyond, no meadowlark declared himself to me from straw-stack or fence-post in the prairie stillness. The blackbirds had all finished their fall conventions on tree and bush, fence and telephone wire. From our part of the world, with the first real snowfall, even the crows would migrate. That Demeter had one hell of a lot to answer for!

Maybe it was too late in the afternoon to go all the way to the cave site, I told myself, but the sun contradicted me. Maybe I might get gored if Vonneguts' bull had got loose again, but there he was, swinging his balls in his own enclosure. Maybe Bill was waiting for me out there!

He wasn't.

If there was ever a war later on, they'd probably shoot me for not going over the top!

I picked out the rosebush first and then a black blot of

raw earth. They'd filled it in! It had never once occurred to
me that they would have filled it in by now! I stood for long
moments, looking down at where it had been, doming now
like the new grave of some prairie giant. In time the earth
would settle and the prairie would heal over its own scar.

If my father ever let me play hockey again, I'd practise
to beat hell, and catch up with the other guys.

When I got back to Sixth, Daisy and Aileen and Ruby
were still taking up the whole sidewalk, but they'd quit
their jacks, and now a skipping-rope was lisping as Daisy
darted in and out like a garter-snake's tongue.

> *"Charlie Chaplin,*
> *Went to France.*
> *Teach the ladies*
> *How to dance.*
> *When he got there*
> *Sat on a pin.*
> *How many inches*
> *Did it go in?*
> *One—two—three—four...."*

Musgrave said it was a dirty skipping song. Daisy's
Dutch bob flapped up and down and her cheeks were bouncing.
"... ten—eleven—twelve—thirteen—*pepper!*"
Under her blouse she really had them bouncing too! She
probably had hair on it now. Maybe Musgrave was right for
once.

XIV

My father did a story in *The Gleaner*, saying that the search for Bill was still on, that Inspector Kydd was quite sure they would soon track him down and bring him to justice. Inspector Kydd suggested that it might be wise for parents to keep their children home from tricks or treats this Hallowe'en, which didn't seem to make so much sense, when further up in the story he had already said that they felt that Bill had quite likely left the district, and the search was going on farther afield.

Peter was speaking to me again, though we were not visiting each other's houses. I had seen King only at a distance, once in the Blue Bird with Eddie Crozier in the end booth. I did not go down there to him. A couple of times I saw him driving by in his McLaughlin with his left arm resting on the top of the door. He was not wearing his black armband for Bella any more.

I guess he pinned on his medals and took part in the Remembrance Day ceremony with other veterans in front of the War Memorial with the girl on tiptoe holding a wreath above the fallen soldier there. I don't know, because we held our own assembly in Sir Walter Raleigh, to honor our boys who had died for us in the war. Before we bowed our heads for three minutes of silence, Angus Hannah recited "The Flag," which is a lot shorter than "Robert Bruce and the Spider."

I got the strap in Mr. Mackey's office again, but it was not my fault. The Liar got it, too. It was not really his fault, either. Before the first bell went that morning, Fat Isbister had come up to me and showed me a round silver cylinder

with a black fur ring on one end. His father had brought it
home to him from the Shriners' convention in Minneapolis,
he said, and if I held it up to my eye I could see the
hootchy-cootchy girl in there. When I said I couldn't see any
hootchy-cootchy girl, he said to turn it around and I did, but
I didn't see her. Later he must have done the same thing with
the Liar because when we went in to our desks, Mr. Mackey
ordered us both into his office and said what is the meaning
of this. The Liar had a black ring around his eye, and I knew
then that I had one too. Mr. Mackey asked why did we do it,
but neither of us told the son-of-a-bitch that it had been put
there by the fur ring Fat had loaded with soot before he came
to school.

That made only two for me for almost a full term. Before
November was over, Peter's score went up to six. He said it
wasn't as bad as caning was. I figured he was lying.

Even though my father and mother seemed to have
eased up about association with Peter, King was still off
limits. The only chance I would have to really see him would
be if the Trojans had a home game on a Friday night and my
father took me. There were two such games scheduled before
Christmas. We saw the second one. I wished I hadn't.

As usual King was the first onto the ice, his thick
goal-stick over his shoulder like a rifle, leading the rest of the
Trojans round the rink, but this time he was not wearing his
old Balaclava. He was not wearing a hockey sweater, either.
He had on his soldier's cap and tunic. He was wearing all his
rainbow ribbons and silver war medals across his chest.

In the first period the Melville Millionaires banged four
goals past him. We got one.

At the start of the second period, when King appeared at
the gate he didn't have his soldier cap on; his medals were
gone, too. He stepped down onto the ice right by where
Sadie Rossdance and some of her girls sat. Sadie was wearing
a black karakul coat just like my mother's and Mrs. Marshall's
and Mrs. Judge Hannah's and Mrs. Sinclair's and Mrs. Crozier's before and after she went into the Mental. With the
heel of his stick King flipped off Sadie's hat and sent it
looping over the ice. He coasted over to it and without
stopping scooped it up. He did not give it back to her. He put

it on and wore it through the whole second period, half the time sitting on top of the net and swinging his skates when the play was at the other end.

Once when there was a breakaway and the Melville Millionaires right wing came down the ice, King jumped down. He crouched with his legs together and his stick across them, and just as the fellow was ready to let go his shot, King reached up and took off Sadie Rossdance's hat and sailed it right into the fellow's face.

The puck went in.

King was replaced in the third period by Barney Elderfield. The Millionaires got three more goals. The final score was: *thirteen-two.*

The next day was Saturday, when the print shop was always closed. Ten o'clock in the morning I went in the Royal. King was not there. I went in again about two and he was not there. Leon didn't know where he was, and said he hadn't been there all day.

Just before supper I went in again. King was there, under the lacrosse and baseball and hockey pictures with him in every one of them. His head was down and he was carving.

I said, "Hi, King."

He jumped almost as though he'd cut himself and he shoved whatever he was carving onto the shelf under the back of the counter. He looked up, but it was as though he'd never met me before.

"Honor thy father and thy mother!" He yelled it, not so much *at* me as beyond me. It startled the two fellows playing fluke on the first table. Sitting in his barber chair, with one knee over the other, Leon looked up from his Bible.

"Sixth one! Right, Leon?"

Leon looked down to his Bible again.

"How can you do that? If your mother died in the San right after you were born—left you alone with a Methodist son-of-a-bitch even you couldn't honor, Leon. I honor Annie Sheepskin! I honor her! She raised me so I'll honor her! Will that do! Will that get me off the hook on the sixth, Leon?"

Leon didn't lift his crow-wing head from the Bible opened in his lap.

"Him—I defy! And his Methodist God and your Holy Roller unforgiving God too, Leon!"

Leon slapped his Bible shut and got down out of the barber chair.

"Annie said I had the Wendigo in me and Wee-sah-kay-chuck for my uncle! Maybe I did then—maybe I still got the Wendigo in me now! That's Cree, Leon. Look up Satan in your Bible there. Try those Gadarene swine while you're at it!"

The door slapped shut behind Leon. The two fellows hadn't gone back to their game of eight-ball, just stood by the table with the butt end of their cues resting on the floor.

"You fellows are new in town, aren't you," King said, standing up behind the counter. "So let me introduce myself. I am Kingsley Spurgeon Motherwell. That is how I'm called but I am not! I am a red bastard dropped under the kinnikinnick by the river a hundred miles east of here ·in the Moose Mountains—bottom of the Salteaux bull pasture! Annie Sheepskin found me in the sweet grass, sucking on a bitch coyote tit!"

The two men said something to each other and put their cues up in the rack. One of them threw two quarters on the counter.

"Never mind the change."

I went out after them.

When I told Peter about it, he said his father felt King was drinking a lot more because of grief over Bella.

"Do you think what he said just might be true, though? Liquor hits Red Indians much harder than it hits white men."

I told Peter it wasn't true, that it was simply drunk talk and King was probably saying a lot of wild things these days. I told Peter that.

What King had been carving, before he shoved it under the counter, hadn't looked very much like a duck or a goose decoy to me.

Christmas began actually three weeks before the twenty-fifth, in the basement of Knox Presbyterian Church. Daisy Inwards would play Mother Mary in our Sunday-school concert nativity play. Again. Her father was our Sunday-school superintendent. It wasn't a totally subjective casting; Daisy had a very loud voice and did look maternal, since she was an early bloomer and had, for her age, the biggest tits in town.

After four we rehearsed three times a week the first two weeks in December. Angus Hannah and Fat Isbister and I were the three wise hired men. Angus would be pretty busy concert night because he would recite "'Twas the Night Before...," as also would Davie Sawyer and Charlie Ballard and Clara Finlay and Benny MacLeod. There was generally a surfeit of "'Twas the Night Before"s in our town, since it wasn't a predominantly Presbyterian piece and was done in the Anglican, Baptist, Methodist, Lutheran, and Catholic basements as well. Or, rather—also. Every year Mrs. Judge Hannah ran the Christmas concert, which pretty well meant that we'd get Angus doing "Robert Bruce and the Spider" as well as everything else he was to do that night.

After Bob Pinnell had played "The Robin's Return" on the piano, Fat and Angus and I came on with our sheets safety-pinned under our chins and bathrobe cords around our middles. We sat down before a red tissue-paper camp fire glowing from the bulb of a plumber's extension light in its wire cage (supplied by Mr. Nickerson), our broomstick camels grazing against the wall near by.

Fat said, "Lo!"

Angus said, "It is a star!"

I said, "It is the star of the East."

We mounted our camels and we galloped across the stage to Bethlehem and the stable furnished with Catholic hay from Cavanaugh's Livery barn. My gift for the babe in the manger was "frank-incents-an'-meer." Whatever that was. The concert ended with "Robert Bruce and the Spider," then Santa Claus with paper bags of candy and Jap oranges.

In our home we had by then decorated the living room, with special attention to the cuckoo clock, leaving it to the very last and draping it just before the hour would strike. When I was little I used to imagine there was surprise on the cuckoo's face when he popped out and saw what we'd done to his vine leaves and grapes.

The last thing we did was to bring the Christmas tree down from the toy-room closet on the third floor, unwrap it, and pry it apart. It was the same age as I was, made out of shrill green feathers and wires; my father had brought it home in 1913 for my first Christmas. Each year it had molted a little more, but tinsel, and the delicately spiral-ribbed

Christmas candles clutched upright in the little tin claws at the ends of the wire branches, revived it beautifully.

For some reason unknown to me, my mother always gave me presents too young for me. Why should someone who has taken Grade Six and Seven in one year and is starting on plane geometry and Latin not be considered mature enough to have a twenty-two rifle or, by way of compromise, a Little Daisy air gun? I had ached for either of them for almost three years. Lobbidy had already had his for two years. Twenty-two. Why would anyone, in her own words "with the brains to pound sand," give somebody who would be thirteen in March a book called *Sowing Seeds in Danny* by Nellie McClung?

My mother's batting average in gift-giving had never been a good one. Right up till I was eight, she had made middy suits on her sewing-machine and given them to me on birthdays and Christmases. Middy suits! Permissible at the age of four and five and six. At seven—maybe. At eight—inexcusable. Even at four I think I hated those middy suits.

All middy suits were divided into three parts: the broad-collared middy itself, stove-pipe pants, and a waist. The middy had shoelace holes at the neck to receive a scarlet ribbon that was to be tied in a bow knot over the breastbone; in each corner of the broad, flap collar down the back was embroidered a red star. The waist was a white, quilted foundation garment much like a life-jacket which has been on a severe diet—or a corset. There dangled from the front of it two black elastic snub garters; up the back ran fourteen very small buttons so that you pretty well had to share a bedroom with a brother if you wanted to get completely undressed at night or dressed up again in the morning. I was an only child. The waist having been conquered, the pants having been buttoned to the waist, the garters having been retrieved from where they had retreated up the pant legs, the long stockings could be pulled up to be clutched by the girl garters. All other boys in North America wore britches covering their knees, while their stockings were kept up properly. By sealer rings.

From the twenty-fourth of May to harvest, until I was almost nine, I would undress a quarter of a mile from the Mental hole, hide my clothes under a clump of buck brush, then walk the rest of the way over the prairie wool, cacti, and spear grass, naked, to avoid mortification. I was quite unsuccessful. I knew that it was known from the North West Territories to the Montana border that I wore corsets with dingly-dangly garters.

Alone in the living room before daybreak on Christmas morning I opened my presents, then braced myself against finding out what was in the shapeless, holly-spattered parcel from my mother. I was right; it *was* wearing apparel. Gray flannel. I lifted it and shook it out and realized what the sewing-machine had been whining at out in the breakfast room for at least ten days before Christmas.

Time can never dissolve those stunning moments when I held up my first pair of long pants! I was twelve going on thirteen in 1924, when no male wore long pants before the age of eighteen.

I pulled them on over my pajama bottoms and looked down at my no-legs. A balloon was inflating inside me and I had grown one foot. I was taller; I was maler as I stared down the long and unbroken creases "with a wild surmise . . . silent upon a peak in Darien."

I wore them Christmas Day and again all through Boxing Day. After breakfast I went outside and I aimed straight for Musgrave's place, but he wasn't home. Out with his Christmas toboggan, his mother told me, and there was no way I was going to any river bank to slide down in my new gray-flannel long pants, even to see Musgrave's face when he got a good look at them. I said to his mother to tell him a Merry Christmas for me, and I also called one through the archway to Musgrave's grampa sitting in his fumed-oak chair tight up into the corner of their living room by the front window. It was hard to tell whether the poor old man even heard me. He just leaned forward and missed the morning-glory mouth of the spittoon at the bottom of the afghan they'd wrapped round his legs. I don't think Musgrave's mother even noticed I was wearing long pants.

Outside on the street I thought of going to Peter's or Lobbidy's. Instead I turned to go downtown. I wanted King to see me in them.

Even without Musgrave telling me, I knew that King had drunk himself off the hockey team, that for days at a time he never sobered up and there was only Leon to mind the pool hall. Besides barbering, Leon now racked up balls, collected from players, and ran the counter. Being a Holy Roller, I guess he drew the line at taking care of the rummy room and anything else besides poker games that went on back there. But Eddie Crozier was able to handle that for King.

I knew, too, that a month or so after Bella's funeral King had given up their suite in the Walker Block and moved in above the pool hall. Lobbidy told me it was just a large, single room up there, studs and slope rafters, attic-bare. He hadn't even a sink, let alone a toilet or bathtub, so that he must have had to use Leon's sink or the pool-hall toilet. He had a cot with two apple-boxes on end, one by the head of the cot, the other on a kitchen table to hold his kitchen dishes. He had an electric hotplate for cooking on. Lobbidy said he couldn't see it was much better than Mr. Pollock had, sleeping under the counter in his junk-yard office.

Because it was Boxing Day the Royal Pool Hall was closed. There were no footprints in the drift piled at the bottom of the outside stairs between the pool hall and McConkey's Drugs. The snow on every step was unmarred; nor were there any tracks on the landing above.

I knocked. I waited. Nobody said to come in. I knocked again. I waited again. I pushed on the door and it opened. I called to the inside, but nobody answered me. I called out again. I decided I had better close the door and come back later, but as I turned away, I heard it—the sound of someone retching.

"King!"

This time it was quite loud, like someone in distress calling for "Ralph!" Again and again and again. He was on his hands and knees on the floor with his shoulder against the side of the cot at the far end of the room, his back heaving. There was no vomit coming up for him, but the whole room was sour with it.

I dropped beside him and put my arm over his shoulders and held his head up and back with my palm cupping his forehead the way my mother always did for me. It seemed to help him. But I could feel his whole body rippling; not just shivering because it was cold in there and he was bare to the waist—it was as though an electric current were running through his whole body.

I heard a rapping. He still had his shoes on and one toe

was drumming against the linoleum. It sounded just like a dog tilted to one hip and scratching frantically with one hind claw to get at a flea behind his ear, while the effort telegraphed right down to the end of the other hind leg.

"King—we better get you back up onto the cot—under the covers."

I pulled back the quilt and discovered a problem. Not very much of the vomit had made it to the floor. I took the sheets right down and off the end of the bed, then I helped him up.

"Let your head hang over some, King, so you can aim at the floor."

Over in the corner by the door I found another blanket and his long khaki army coat. All his goal equipment was there, too. I brought back the leg pads; they were lined with thick felt, so it was not silly to buckle them on him before I covered him with the blanket and then the army coat.

The Quebec heater was cold, but there was paper and kindling and a scuttle of coal. Once the fire had caught, I went back to him. He was lying on his back and his eyes were closed. He was still shaking but not nearly so much now. I wondered when he had eaten last; it didn't matter one way or the other, really, the way he'd been throwing up. I decided to go down and across the street to Chan Kai's for coffee and hot soup. I had only a dime, but I could just tell Chan it was for King and charge it.

I hadn't even got halfway to the door when he screamed. It made me go cold inside my elbows; it was an all—out Mental scream, the kind we sometimes heard from way inside there when we were on the grounds. He kept winding it up again and again just like the fire whistle on the town hall. I wanted to run out of there, but I didn't. I forced myself over to him where he'd ripped off the blanket and coat and was writhing and clawing at his bare chest and stomach.

"Moving! Moving again!"

He had thrown himself over onto his stomach and was sliding up and down the mattress as though he were trying to rub something off himself.

"Feel every goddam scale! Oh, God!"

I could see the muscles on his back jumping.

"Aaah—wriggling Jesus! Get it off me! Get it off!"

He threw himself round, clutching and scratching at his

crotch, at his stomach—his chest. Then I saw why. His serpent had come alive. I could see it undulate all the way up his belly, coiling over his chest, the arrow head wavering and the forked tongue flickering at the hollow in the side of his throat. He grabbed at his neck.

"Don't let her! Don't! Oh, please—don't...!"

"Get out!" It was Eddie Crozier behind me.

"No! No!..."

"Go on home, kid!" He pushed me out of the way.

"Not—her—poison kiss!"

Eddie slid an arm under King's shoulders to lift him. He put a bottle up to King's mouth and tilted it for him.

I got out.

That evening just before I went to bed my father said, "You didn't get to this one, Hugh—after you opened your long pants." He was holding out a parcel wrapped in store paper, tied with string. "Eddie Crozier dropped it into the shop last week."

It was a little blue-wing teal decoy.

Having my first pair of long pants was no longer very important to me.

As it seemed to every year, an early March blizzard howled down on my birthday. By noon the town dray, the mill dray, and Aitken's Coal and Wood drays were lined up in front of Sir Walter Raleigh to take us all home, so that we wouldn't lose direction and wander out onto the prairie and freeze to death in a snowdrift. The blizzard should have buggered up the birthday party my mother had planned for after four that afternoon, but it didn't.

No guests came through forty below and driving snow, but we had a birthday party all the same, just my father and mother and I, while the wind raged wild outside, and inside dirged like a mouth organ, through the brass and felt weatherstripping on the storm windows. We celebrated in the dining room under the crystal chandelier winking and blinking from the thirteen yellow birthday candles, which I blew out with one breath. In front of the fireplace I opened my presents: tube skates, a Gilbert's Magic Set, and the *Chums* my mother should have got me instead of *Sowing Seeds in Danny* at Christmas.

My father must have wanted the last present I opened to be the last one. When I had unwrapped it and lifted the cardboard lid off it and saw it folded there, I yelled.

My father said, "Might be too small for you—see if it fits."

I climbed into it and pulled it up. It fit. Over my pants. Johnson and Johnson. My first jockstrap!

"I guess you can go to hockey practice at the Arena now," my father said.

My mother cried.

I slept with it under my pajamas that night.

Because the blizzard was still blowing, there was no school all next day. Who cared! I practised magic tricks and got really good at making the cherries grow one by one between my fingers and then disappear. I wore my jockstrap all day. And that night. And the next day at school. And the next.

I knew why my father had relented about hockey; Musgrave had been the first to tell me that Barney Elderfield was coaching the Trojan Juniors as well as playing goal for the Seniors. On Saturday King was not in the Arena to see the goal I almost scored against the Tiger Lily Hounds. Or my jockstrap.

After the game, Musgrave came over to me by the stove in the dressing room.

"You got that jockstrap for your birthday."

"Mmm-hmh."

"I bet you haven't had it off ever since."

I didn't tell him he would have won his bet.

"Wearing it all the time will weaken your balls, you know."

Not until later did I think of an answer for him, and by school on Monday, when I saw him next, it was too late to tell him how lucky he was to have very strong balls because he didn't have a jockstrap at all!

Since my father was letting me play hockey again I assumed that quite likely he did not care too much about whether or not I saw King Motherwell. So I went to the room above the pool hall again.

This time I don't know how many times I knocked on his door and there was no answer at all.

I knocked and I waited and I knocked and I waited, then I knocked really hard and loud. I knew he was in there and that he could hear me! Why did he refuse to come to the door or to call out to me? I didn't want to go in where I wasn't wanted! Leave that to Musgrave! King hadn't liked it very much when Bill was down in our cave, stubborn and refusing to let us help him when he needed us! King had *smoked* him out of there!

I got halfway down the stairs before I turned around and went right back up and inside. As soon as I stepped in I could hear him, a low, muttering sound that went on and on.

His voice was strangely cadenced, rising and falling like wind through long grass, starting and stopping and starting up again unexpectedly. It wasn't talking, really, for there were no distinguishable words being shaped by lips and tongue. It seemed to be all in the throat and not all that different from what I'd heard the Holy Rollers do, writhing on the river bank when Blind Jesus had walked across the water to them.

King had a blanket gathered round his shoulders. He was sitting on the cot with his legs crossed and his back up into the corner of the wall. His eyes were closed.

"King—you all right, King?"

He went right on sing-songing, his head rocking from side to side, and he was not in the room with me at all. It was somebody else's voice that kept fluttering up out of King.

It died away. The rocking movement stopped.

"I got my own! I got my own!"

His eyes were open now.

"Can't take it from me!"

He was not seeing me.

"Annie told me! She told me!"

He began to rock and chant again. This wasn't as bad as he'd been on my visit on Boxing Day, when he'd had the shakes so violently that his snake was coiling and he screamed about the poison kiss. But still, I wished that I weren't up there with him.

He was holding up something that looked like a scrotum gathered together at the top, and I smelled a faint smoke smell. Buckskin.

"Red! Mine's red!"

He wasn't making any sense at all. I knew there wasn't

anything I could do for him and that Leon was below in the pool hall in case King got worse. At least, I told myself that as I left him. Just as I went out the door, I heard him again.

"To hell with Bible medicine! My cousins hang their hearts on trees!"

I was halfway home when I realized that the little bag he'd been holding must be a medicine bag.

XV

Holgar Petersen found Bill's body May Day, in the pool where warm water from the Mental powerhouse first thawed out the Little Souris in spring. Holgar had been looking for the carcass of a lump-jaw steer of his that had gone missing a week before. He found Bill first, with an iron harrow wheel haywired to one ankle. King was arrested five days later, after the inquest. He was tried for the murder of Bill in the Spring Assizes.

Everyone felt sorry for King; after all, he had only done the thing they wished they might be able to do if a madman beat their wife to death. And most of them knew they couldn't have. Judge Hannah and the jury must have felt the same about it, for they found King not guilty by reason of insanity. King was taken out to the Mental to join Horny Harold and Buffalo Billy and Blind Jesus and Mrs. Eddie Crozier—for the rest of his life.

I never saw King again. Once they took him to the Mental, he had no visitors at all. It was not because they would not let him have visitors, I heard my father tell my mother, but because he did not want any. He refused to see anyone at all. I went out there a few times, and I walked around the north wing where they had Ward Four, the bad one, where Bill had spent most of his time before his last escape. I did it only once. I didn't tell Peter I had looked up at the barred windows and tried to guess which one might be King's. I wondered about the possibility of King's escaping. He could have done it—easily. If he had, Peter and I could have helped him; we could have hidden him the way we did Bill. I didn't mention that to Peter either.

The fall after King entered the Mental, Blind Jesus go
spattered against the cow-catcher of the northbound Soo Line
passenger out of Minneapolis-St. Paul.

"I saw him clear in plenty of time," the engineer said in
my father's interview for *The Gleaner* front-page story on "*
Sad Event.*" "But I couldn't believe what I seen! Long-haired
guy in a white robe, his arms stretched right out sideways
his face and that beard tipped up! That late in the day the sun
was low, like coming from behind the train. There was a
cloud bank low on the horizon west, behind, and we're
high-balling east making up time. There was those streaky
bars from all the straw-stacks burning this time of the year
He wasn't real!"

By the time the engineer realized that Blind Jesus *was*
real and applied the brakes, it was too late. "Reason we were
shovelling on the coal, we lost time earlier. Same morning we
hit an antelope too," he explained. "Just east of Grassy Lake."

It should have happened sooner, for almost a month
before, Vonneguts' Holstein bull had got away from Raoul
who was leading him over to Tinchers' to service their cow
herd. Buffalo Billy never galloped again, paralyzed from the
waist down after one of the bull's horns had severed his spinal
cord.

I came home when my father died in the summer of
1937. I went with my mother to Orrin Nightingale's Funeral
Home. Mr. Nightingale withdrew after he had ushered u
into the cool and fragrant slumber room. It smelled not so
much of lilies and carnations as it did of apples. I thought of
the root cellar below our basement stairs.

My father lay in an oak and bronze casket in the center
of the dim room, stilled with the dreadful and unconcerned
patience of death. I had never seen him in life with those
small hands cupped over each other and against the front of
him. I had seen him in sleep, but now death or Mr. Nightin
gale seemed to have domed his eyes. Against the frilled and
pleated white satin he did not look small at all.

It was not my father.

My father was the bonfire smell of cigar smoke, cheek
stubble male and harsh against the side of my face, the man
who wrote the dog obituaries one after the other in *The*

Gleaner throughout the summer that the poisoner got nine-
een with strychnine in meat chunks. He was the man who
inally said to my mother, "I change my goddam socks and
inderwear just as often as I change my typewriter ribbon!"
My father taught me to read at four. He pulled the leather
aces snug on my skates, and he rubbed the circulation back
nto my aching feet after I had skated too long on the Little
Souris ice. He tilted my chin in the bathroom and squeezed
out the drops when I had pinkeye.

This was not my father.

My father bought me my first jockstrap on my thirteenth
birthday. He clearly explained square root to me after Mr.
Mackey had strapped me three times for refusing to get it
right up at the board. He kept telling me, "Don't eat that,
Elmer," and he told Inspector Kydd to his face that Russian
wolfhounds were stupid. He was the only one who always
called me "Hugh." I did not have to defend my interior from
my father.

This was not my father.

I saw that the fingernails of each small hand had curved
black margins. The knuckles were in mourning, too, for they
still had ink threads, defeating death and Mr. Nightingale and
my mother.

Then I cried for my father, and for myself.

That summer was not an easy time for either my mother
or me, not only because of our grief, but because with the
years we had both lost some of the small talent we'd ever had
for patience. My mother still tended to come on too strong,
right through neutral territory and into my own. She could
not understand why I should want to go three times running
in August to the Yellow Grass weekend dance, especially with
Sally Gibson, who was just an attendant out at the Mental,
instead of any one of a number of other girls she could think
of. I did not tell my mother that they probably would not
care to go to a Yellow Grass dance either. Nor did I tell her
the candidates she could think of would not be at all interested in coming with me to Brokenshell Grove after the Yellow
Grass Silver Tone Seven had played "Save the Last Dance for
Me, Sweetheart." I was extremely careful after visiting
McConkey's Drugstore to keep them in a mason jar on the
earth shelf of the old root cellar under the basement stairs.
Before the summer was over and I could return to Victoria

College, I rather wished that the three little Sadie Rossdance cottages did not now stand empty out beyond the Fairgrounds.

Now my mother lived on the ground floor of our house, converted into her own self-contained suite with the old music room for her bedroom. The breakfast room had become her kitchen, so that she no longer needed the dumb waiter. Like the rest of the basement the downstairs kitchen had become a storage area for trunks and cartons of stored possessions belonging to the suite people. A new young doctor and his wife rented the second-floor apartment, and the collegiate chemistry teacher had the top one. I slept in the spare room which had once been my father's den.

My father had done most of the renovation himself, my mother said, in two years of his spare time, and with professional help only for the outside staircase that angled up the north wall of the house. The oak English-billards table without pockets, its slates crated, was stored in the garage. It was to be mine. My father had donated the billiard-room furniture to the new Elks' Hall.

"I ordered it for him," my mother said, "when we bought the house from Mr. Humphrey. I didn't know he hated it." I did not tell her that I had too.

My mother had another surprise for me when she told me she was not selling the print shop; she had made an arrangement with Alex Wachovic that he would run it, paying rent for the building and the presses and linotype as well as monthly increments against the purchase of the *Gleaner* circulation and printing goodwill. With all that and the rent from the two suites, she would have no financial worries.

"What's his name?"

"Alex Wachovic. He's worked for your father the past three years." I did not know him, and this was the first time I'd known that my father had hired anyone to help him.

"You wouldn't know him. His people farmed near Cedoux. Polish. He married a Vonnegut girl. The oldest one, I think."

My mother also told me that Angus Hannah was at Oxford, having won a Rhodes scholarship. He had turned into a fine young debater and had graduated magna cum laude from McGill in Political Science. Two of the Chans, Edward and Kathleen, had taken the Governor General's medal on graduating to collegiate from Sir Walter Raleigh School.

Austin Musgrave was head cashier in the Royal Bank. I had received this information from her before. In letters.

I did not run across Musgrave till almost three weeks after my father's funeral. We met as he came out of Crozier's Men's Wear and I was on my way to the Soo Beer Parlor. He turned down my invitation to have a beer with me, suggesting instead a coffee at the Blue Bird Cafe. The Liar, he said, was a beer-slinger in the Soo, and I said, yes, I knew that.

"An alcoholic as well."

In the Blue Bird he told me that Lobbidy was quite successful now. Financially. Long before the Depression hit, Lobbidy's father had changed the livery stable to a taxi business and also set up a slaughter-house. Lon had inherited both, sold the taxi stand, and started a silver-fox farm east of town, feeding the foxes with the entrails and horse meat from the slaughter-house. He had three children already, the first one seven years old, born three months after Lobbidy had married Daisy Inwards. He also bred trotting horses. Daisy had not turned. My mother had written me none of this information.

I congratulated Musgrave on doing so well in the bank.

"Just a means to an end. I have no strong banking ambitions. I've been doing correspondence courses from McMaster University."

"Divinity school?" McMaster was of course a Baptist university.

"Psychology. Abnormal. I've been saving, and by next year I'll be able to go down east for a full academic year. I didn't inherit or have it easy."

Like me and Angus Hannah and Lobbidy. "I understand Angus is at Oxford on a Rhodes scholarship."

"In kilts!"

That was rather good for Musgrave. I said, "How's your grampa?"

"You know he died five years after..."

It was Musgrave who did not care to complete the sentence. I had known. Also I knew that the poor old man had never once gone out to get lost after we blew him up in the Musgrave backhouse. He was afraid to go wandering and spitting down the street, with his cane and his Mountie hat and his knapsack on. Thinking of all those years Musgrave had emptied spittoons and gone looking for his grampa, I was not surprised that he should be taking correspondence courses from McMaster in abnormal psychology.

"I suppose you've noticed a lot of changes," Musgrave said.

"Not really."

"The Sadie Rossdance cottages are empty now."

"I did notice that."

"Two years ago she just pulled out. In quite a hurry. She left everything—rugs, drapes, sheets, towels, furniture—pianos—behind her."

"Did she."

He lowered his voice. "About a month after one of her girls died."

I thought of asking him which one, but he'd probably know. "Where'd she go?"

"Whores follow wealth. Calgary. Even with the Depression there's cattle and oil money in Calgary. She goes under the name of Pearl White now, has a fancy mansion in the Mount Royal district."

"Musgrave, will you tell me something. I have wanted to know for years. Just how the hell do you manage to find out all the things you do—about other people?" I waited. "Can you prove to me that Sadie Rossdance—under the name of Pearl White—is running a fancy Calgary cat-house?"

"Yes."

"Oh." I waited. "Do it then." I waited some more. "You've been in it."

"Two years ago I was made head cashier at the bank."

"Is that relevant?"

He looked over his shoulder both ways. "She had a windfall. She . . . " He stopped as someone passed behind us. "She made a twenty-thousand-dollar deposit late on a Friday afternoon—just before closing. First thing Monday morning she withdrew it, mostly as a transfer to our main Calgary branch. Eighth Avenue. She left on the Soo Line train two o'clock that afternoon." He lifted his cup, then put it back on the saucer without taking a sip. "Blackmail."

"You guess."

"Uh-uh. I know."

"Who blackmailed her?"

"*She* did the blackmailing!"

"Of whom?"

"Dr. Sinclair."

"You are kidding!"

"Abortion."

"How can you possibly know—!"

"Sshhhh! Sinclair made a twenty-thousand withdrawal—or rather, a twelve-thousand-dollar one from his account, and signed a note for eight more on the Thursday." Austin Musgrave, still the information witcher; what a pity his forked hazel wand could douse only foul water!

"I suppose you know—King Motherwell hanged himself."

"Yes."

"Tore his hospital gown into strips and tied them together. From the heating duct in the Mental tunnel. Poor man." The sick void within me was just as bad as it had ever been. "I felt real sorry for you and Peter—that summer, you know. You want another cup?"

"No."

"Me either. I drink too much of it. I was pretty sure about that cave of yours—I was pretty hurt, too, the way you and Peter kept me out of it—I don't suppose King meant to get you fellows into all that trouble—Bill the Sheepherder." He was leaving pauses to give me a chance to say something. I did not care to use them. "Bella—she's the one that ruined him—married her right out of Sadie Rossdance's. Herbie Millican—you remember—used to work in McConkey's Drugstore? Herbie saw all the prescriptions went through there. He told me what Bella gave King for a nice wedding present."

"All right, Musgrave. . . ."

"Huh?"

"I promise."

"What—"

"Not to play with the Liar or Angus or Lobbidy ever again—or King." He knew instantly and exactly what I meant, but it did not stop him.

"I didn't care who you played with—or got into trouble with! I could have saved you and Deane-Cooper a lot of grief! I'll tell you something else about Motherwell, too! Judge Hannah—the jury—they never did get it right about Bill the Sheepherder, and Bella and him!"

Now I knew what Musgrave had been leading up to ever since we'd come into the Blue Bird. I also knew what I had been leading up to.

"You kept me out of your cave!"

"Only because you were such a prick, Musgrave—and still are! "

Then I hit him. I suppose I took unfair advantage of him, doing it in the Blue Bird, but if I had waited till we were outside he would have had room to run.

Even now the memory shames me a little. After all, he did make it to McMaster the next year, joined the South Saskatchewan Regiment the winter of 1940, moved on through warrant officer to a captaincy in Ottawa, and by the end was high up in army personnel-testing there. After the war he got his doctorate under the veterans' plan. Today he practises in Portland or Seattle or San Francisco, if he has not retired. Give Musgrave credit; he could have settled for less, like winning the Boston Marathon. I have no excuse for under-estimating him, for I was there in the Musgrave back yard early summer of 1924 when we blew up his grampa in their backhouse. It was inevitable that he should become Dr. Austin Musgrave, a fellow Canadian of whom we should all be proud, responsible, though he would deny it, at the age of twelve for the world's first use of shock therapy on the mentally ill.

I can just imagine an analysis session with Austin in Seattle or Portland or San Francisco after his receptionist, Miss Cromwell, has said, "Dr. Musgrave will penetrate you now."

I can see his narrow face, not so much solicitous as eager. Yes! That's it! Just like a fox terrier anxious at the burrow tunnel mouth, waiting for those gophers of fear and guilt and shame to be drowned out when the last washtub of slough water has been tipped down and the final bubble of air has wobbled to the surface.

"You simply have not accepted my invitation. Since our last session you have spilled your seed upon the ground as well as playing with face cards instead of the clean, new deck of Old Maid cards I gave you. You also went to a circus, a

picture show, a dance. How can I possibly help you if you persist in shooting pea pool, in holding back your Sunday-school and Mission Band collection for the wicked purchase of licorice whips, pipes, plugs, and cigars. Right now I can see by your black tongue and the corners of your lips that you have been sucking jaw-breakers. I suspect that you still have fried-egg candies in your pocket.

"I will level with you. Satan rules one half of the world— more likely nine-tenths—and there is only one way to redemption from your anguish and torment: total immersion. Soap for all orifices—mouth, ears, nose, rectum, vagina. No remission otherwise. In your case I cannot be optimistic. Prognosis: Hell. So—same time next week. I will walk with you and I will talk with you and I will enter to bring help to you. Just tell Ursula on your way out. And don't forget to do your umbilicus and your foreskin."

I had thought that Austin was the only victim. All of us were. We simply hadn't noticed the adult footprints in our child caves, but they were there all the time, left by guardian trespassers. They entered uninvited because they loved us and they feared for us. Often they entered only to tidy up for us, or simply out of curiosity to find out what we might be doing in there. They wanted only to make it safe for their vulnerable young, to clear it of danger. They did not know, nor did we, that they could be carriers, unintentionally leaving serpents behind, coiled in a dark corner, later to bite and poison and destroy.

Poor Austin!

Poor Liar with his bottle of McGoof in a brown paper bag, seeking shelter under a cardboard carton in some Cabbagetown alley!

Poor Angus eating up all that Bruce and the Spider horse shit!

Poor Peter shot down in the Battle of Britain!

Poor King!

Poor me!

I will never be even with Austin. I hit him too late that day in the Blue Bird, after he had started to tell me something about King and Bella and Bill. I should not blame Austin, really, for I should have known what I have refused to know all these years. I knew King better than anybody *else, better than the jurors, better than Judge Hannah. From the day that I saw Sadie Rossdance and her girls come down to swim, I knew that Bella was going out to the three little cottages whenever King was away on his runs over the border. I was the one who found Bella with her head like a bruised and bloodied nail keg. I was the one who caught a glimpse of what King was carving out of sight behind the counter in the Royal Pool Hall, the winter of 1924.*

I do not know who got the rest of King's decoys, but after he hanged himself in the Mental tunnel, my father sent me one of them to join the little blue-wing teal. King gave me the Christmas I got my first pair of long pants. I suppose it was the last carving he ever did: the statue of a lovely naked woman, her black hair hanging free. She is stained red, with pin-cherry juice I suspect. Her right cheek, from the corner of her nose down past the corner of her mouth, has a long scar seam.

I had always known that King could never have killed Bill, after he had given him sanctuary in our cave and bathed him and fed him and given him the little bum lamb. I know that King found him dead down there after the silver plate had given Bill one fit too many. I think King had a pretty good notion that Bella was going back to Sadie Rossdance's whenever he made his runs down into Montana, but when he found out about Mrs. Inspector Kydd it was too much for him. I was the one who told King about our tea-wagon tipped in the living-room archway, and about how Mrs. Inspector Kydd began to visit Bella in the Walker Block regularly after that, to spy on us. He must have beaten the lovely whore to death in a drunken rage of frustration. Only that could have explained the way Bella's head was when I found her in our cave mouth.

When he discovered Bill dead from one last, great seizure in our cave, King must have hauled him out, wired the harrow wheel to an ankle, and dumped him in the Little Souris. Then he put Bella's body into the cave. Perhaps he hoped that people would think that Bill had dug the cave to hide himself, just as Peter had said they would if I hadn't told my father. After he had found Bill dead, it would be quite natural for King to use Bill as a decoy, and it would not be a dishonorable thing for him to do.

Finally I may have it sorted out.

Now my summer holidays are over.
I wish I had not told him about Mrs. Inspector Kydd and
the pink dress!
I hope that he has haunted me for love!

ABOUT THE AUTHOR

W. O. MITCHELL was born in Weyburn, Saskatchewan, in 1914. Although he has lived most of his life in Alberta and Saskatchewan, he has travelled widely and has been a lifeguard, deckhand, salesman, and high school teacher. For many years he was the most renowned resident in High River, Alberta, but he now lives in Calgary. He is in great demand as a visiting professor (currently at the University of Windsor) and as a performer reading from his works.

Of these, his best-loved book is *Who Has Seen the Wind*. Since its publication in 1947 it has sold over a quarter of a million copies in Canada alone and is hailed as the great Canadian classic of boyhood. His other works include *Jake and the Kid* (based on his legendary CBC Radio series) and his most recent book, *The Vanishing Point*. He also adapted another novel, *The Kite*, for the stage, where its immense success matched that of *Back to Beulah*, which is soon to be a motion picture.

Mr. Mitchell was made an Officer of the Order of Canada in 1973, and has been the subject of an NFB documentary. He is, in Pierre Berton's words, "an original."

THE MANAWAKA SERIES

by

Margaret Laurence

Canada's celebrated novelist and Winner Of The Governor-General's Award

The Manawaka stories, set in the most famous fictional town in Canada, offer a clear-eyed vision of Canadian land and people. Canada's most popular storyteller balances humor and pathos as she portrays the human condition through characters struggling to come to terms with themselves and with the world. Laurence fans can find all of these heart-warming novels now in paperback, at all good bookstores throughout Canada.

41833-3	STONE ANGEL	$3.95
42002-8	A JEST OF GOD	$3.95
42039-7	FIRE DWELLERS	$3.95
42045-1	DIVINERS	$4.50
42069-9	BIRD IN THE HOUSE	$3.95

THE MARK OF CANADIAN BESTSELLERS

FIVE BY

MITCHELL

A sophisticated thinker, playwright, raconteur and creative teacher, W. O. Mitchell writes novels of innocence overwhelmed by experience in his fictional documentaries of Canadian small-town life.

His first book, WHO HAS SEEN THE WIND is a permanent Canadian classic. A work of brilliance, sheer beauty and rare perception, this tells of a child's search for "the ultimate meaning of the cycle of life."

In JAKE AND THE KID Mitchell shows his special skill in capturing the peculiar individuality of his characters. This is the story of a hired man, a ten-year old boy and their homely, whimsical adventures.

THE VANISHING POINT presents the complex dilemma of native peoples and the well-meaning whites who try to help them. Much of the power of this novel lies in the rendering of the Indian characters, authentic and strong.

Remarkable for its descriptive beauty, humour and original characterization, THE KITE is written with vitality and affection, and will warm the reader's heart in its presentation of time and old age.

What begins as a dream of boyhood in HOW I SPENT MY SUMMER HOLIDAYS ends in a nightmare of corruption and insanity. Most somber of Mitchell's novels, this is a haunting, powerful tale of lost innocence.

 Available in Seal paperbacks at all good bookstores throughout Canada.